Wedding Bells in Silverwood

Other books by Dorothy Dreyer

Silverwood Series

Christmas in Silverwood

Black Mariah series

Black Mariah: Hanau, Germany

Curse of the Phoenix series

Phoenix Descending
Paragon Rising

Empire of the Lotus Series

Crimson Mage
Copper Mage
Golden Mage
Emerald Mage
Sapphire Mage
Amethyst Mage
Diamon Mage

Blade Bound Saga

A Dagger in the Ivy

Awards

2018 New Apple Award for Outstanding Young Adult Fantasy

Wedding Bells in Silverwood

DOROTHY
DREYER

Wedding Bells in Silverwood

This is a work of fiction. Names, characters, places, and incidents either are the product of the author's imagination or are used fictitiously.
Any resemblance to actual persons, living or dead, or locales is entirely coincidental.

Cover design by Michael J. Canales
www.MJCImageworks.com

ISBN: 978-1-64548-057-0

Published by Rosewind Romance
An imprint of Vesuvian Books
www.RosewindRomance.com

Printed in the United States

10 9 8 7 6 5 4 3 2 1

For Kovu and Kascha
I miss you both every day

Chapter One

Did I really agree to this?

Holly St. Ives shielded her eyes from the August sun and glared at the uphill dirt trail in front of her, half tempted to fake a sudden illness so she could go home and hide under the covers. She'd prefer her nice, warm, cozy bed to a thin sleeping bag on a cold, bumpy tent floor anyway.

Nick Mason, her devoted boyfriend for eight months and counting, closed the SUV's trunk and roped his arms through the straps of the oversized backpack. "You ready for this?"

Nick's Alaskan Malamute, Cupid, wagged his tail eagerly, waiting for the green light to charge up the hill.

Holly eyed the steep climb and raised her brow. "Would you be upset if I changed my mind?"

Nick handed Holly her rucksack, which was considerably smaller than his. "I thought you said seeing the Northern Lights is at the top of your bucket list."

Holly squirmed as she slung the pack over her thin jacket. "I could just watch them online." She yanked her chestnut brown waves out from the purple, pashmina scarf encompassing her neck, hoping Nick might agree with her.

Nick smirked, rubbing a hand over the scruff on his chiseled jawline. "That's not the same thing."

"I know." Holly shifted, kicking a rock with her hiking boots. "But when you invited me on this trip, I didn't realize how much we'd be … roughing it."

Nick placed his hands on her hips and tugged her close. "Look, once we get up there and have everything set up, you'll love it. I booked a premium spot, one the park assured me was a perfect place to experience the aurora borealis. And if that's not enough to tempt you, I've brought hot chocolate and marshmallows."

Holly swayed, adjusting the weight she carried. "Like mini marshmallows that go in the hot chocolate or big ones for roasting over a fire?"

"Both."

Holly squinted at him with a half-smile. "Fine. But only because I'm a sucker for cocoa." *And the company's not so bad either.*

Cupid barked, reminding them he was still waiting for permission to start their adventure. The black and white bundle of fur sniffed at the air and paced around Nick.

"Yeah, go on, boy." Nick grasped the tent bag handles as Cupid took off and then gave Holly a quick peck before pulling a cap over his short-cropped, dark hair.

With a sigh of defeat, Holly gathered her waves into a quick, messy bun. *You can do this. It'll be worth it. Just think of those magical lights.*

Holly marveled at Nick's prowess as he effortlessly maneuvered through the challenging terrain. His sinewy frame flexed with every step, the ripple of well-defined muscles subtly evident beneath the fabric of his plaid shirt. With each confident stride, Nick expertly balanced the heavy backpack on his broad shoulders and held the gear in his grip, the weight seemingly inconsequential to his hardy physique. His movements were graceful and purposeful, a testament to his physical and mental strength.

The national park enveloped the young couple in a breathtaking tapestry of natural beauty. Towering evergreens reached toward the sky, their branches swaying gently in the late summer breeze, creating a soothing symphony of rustling leaves. Sunlight filtered through the thick foliage, casting dappled patterns on the forest floor.

The air was warm but invigorating, scented with the earthy pine perfume and wildflowers' delicate fragrance. A chorus of chirping birds provided a melodic soundtrack, their songs echoing through the tranquil wilderness. The occasional flutter of wings and the rustle of small animals in the underbrush added a touch of lively energy to the scene's serenity.

A few minutes into their ascent, Holly's city-girl nature became apparent. The path twisted and turned, leading them through dense foliage and steep inclines. Her backpack weighed heavier as the day grew hotter. Was it necessary to lug all the extra layers of clothes up the mountain in the summer heat when all she wanted to do was fall into a pool and cool off? She huffed and puffed, trying to keep up with Nick's confident strides. It wasn't as if she'd never hiked before. In the quaint, snow-covered mountain town of Silverwood, which Holly officially called home for the last year, she would often follow the trail near her cabin for a hike. But this trek proved more challenging, especially with the equipment she carried, and she lagged behind.

"Are you sure this is the right way?" Holly struggled to get the words out between her labored breath. She wiped the sweat from her temples and then rubbed her damp palms on her jeans. She may have mastered the art of strutting through New York in heels, but this rugged terrain turned out to be more difficult than she'd anticipated. "We couldn't drive uphill somehow?"

"The spot I booked isn't designated for a vehicle." Nick glanced at her over his shoulder, a coy grin on his lips. "You're doing great. It's not far now."

Holly swatted at a mosquito. "I have a feeling your definition of 'far' is very different from mine. And why do I feel like these mosquitoes are only attacking *me*?"

"They probably smell your fear," Nick joked.

Holly smacked her neck, hoping she'd eliminated at least one of the flying miscreants. "That's not fear they smell. It's sw—" Before she could finish her sentence, her eyes landed on something long, thin, and slithery in the underbrush.

Panic seized her heart, and she released a loud shriek that frightened nearby birds from the trees. She stumbled backward, her arms flailing. Her palm grazed a prickly bush, and its thorns sliced into her skin. A sharp cry escaped her throat when she lost her footing and slid into a patch of mud. She gasped as warm wetness seeped into her jeans.

Cupid's barks filled the air as he charged to her aid.

Nick quickly doubled back and rushed to her side. "Holly! What happened?"

Wide-eyed, Holly pointed to where she'd seen the horrid creature. "A snake! There's a snake."

Cupid sniffed around the area she indicated.

Holly cradled her injured hand. "Nick, get Cupid away from there." Her voice rose as fear strangled her vocal cords.

Nick helped Holly to her feet and gingerly took her hand in his. "First, let me see." He hissed at the sight of blood welling in her palm, then removed the bandana that was tied to his backpack, wrapping it around her injury. "We can clean and wrap it better once we get to the campsite."

Holly stiffened as Cupid moved closer to the threat. "He's going to get attacked."

"I don't think there are any snakes around here, but I'll check." Nick walked over to the area, his eyes narrowed.

Holly sucked in a breath as he reached the spot and leaned

forward. When Nick straightened, he bit back a laugh. Cupid lifted his head, a long stick clenched in his teeth.

Holly swallowed hard. "I swear it was a snake."

Nick returned to her side and rubbed a hand over her back. "Nature can be tricky. But that stick's not going to hurt you."

"I wouldn't be too sure," Holly mumbled.

"Well, Cupid's got it under control now, so you don't have to worry."

Holly wiped her muddy, uninjured hand on the dry part of her jeans and gave in to the humor of the situation, relieved she hadn't had to deal with a reptile bite. With a snicker, she tilted her head. "Just what you had in mind, right? I'm the perfect date. At the first hill, I started hallucinating, and now I'm covered in sweat, mud, and blood. I'm just a big mess."

Nick tugged her closer by her waist and gazed at her, the deep blue of his eyes locked on the warm brown of hers. "You're my mess."

Holly let out a small laugh in response right before Nick kissed her lips lightly.

"Now, let's get up to the campsite, City Girl," Nick said, "so I can take a proper look at that cut in your hand."

Holly couldn't wait to get out of her filthy jeans. The summer sun had helped to dry some of the caked-on mud, but she was far from comfortable. They'd been walking for what felt like hours, and she began to wonder if the Northern Lights were worth the effort.

"We're almost there, right?" She had to take a breath between words.

"Yeah." Nick smiled at her over his shoulder. "Not far now."

They reached level ground, and Holly spotted a camper standing proudly amidst the wilderness. An orange and white striped awning extended from its side unfurled like a welcoming embrace from the cheerful abode on wheels. The awning stretched outward, its sturdy fabric creating a shaded oasis. Beneath it, a weathered picnic table rested, adorned with a bright yellow tablecloth that danced in the breeze. Surrounding the table were four lightweight folding chairs. Two young boys sat nearby, one on his phone and the other reading a comic book. The delicious aroma of a home-cooked meal wafted through the air from one of the camper windows.

That didn't seem too bad. "Will our tent look anything like that when it's done?" Holly clasped her hands together under her chin.

Nick glanced past her. "Not exactly. That's a camper. Our setup is a bit more rustic."

Holly pursed her lips. "Oh."

The sound of their boots crunching against the trail helped Holly concentrate on something other than her damp clothes and her heavy backpack. The camper they'd passed earlier was now far behind them and downhill.

Finally, as they rounded a bend, they reached a clearing.

The picturesque glade overlooked a breathtaking vista of majestic, snow-capped mountains, and wildflowers adorned the meadows, painting the landscape with vibrant splashes of pink, purple, and yellow. The sunset provided a tranquil backdrop, with dragonflies zipping toward the lake and birds leaping from tree to tree.

Nick stopped, gripped the straps of his backpack, and gave Holly a wide grin. "We're here."

She raised a hand to her chest, fingers lightly brushing her collarbone, while a soft exhale escaped her lips. "This is gorgeous."

"I told you it would be worth it." Nick set his gear on the ground and unpacked the tent poles.

Cupid found a place to settle nearby, chewing on the stick he carried from their hike.

The area was surrounded by long grass that swished in the wind. Holly welcomed the breeze, closing her eyes momentarily as it cooled her hot and sweaty skin. She let the tranquility settle over her, its calmness washing away the strain of the hike and easing every lingering thought from her mind.

Aluminum poles clinked together and roused her from her reverie. Nick had made impressive progress erecting their tent.

She slipped the pack from her shoulders and drew nearer. "Can I help?"

"Sure. Can you hand me that pole there?" Nick jutted his chin and pointedly looked at the spot he meant as he stretched out the canvas.

Holly bent down to retrieve the item he'd requested with her bandana-wrapped hand. "This one?"

"No, the one next to it."

Holly sighed. "If you think I know what I'm doing, you're in for a surprise. I never put up a tent when I lived in New York."

He took the pole she handed him. "What about when you were a kid? You came to Silverwood every year."

"Yeah, in the winter." She scoffed. "Not exactly camping season."

"I don't know if I agree with that." Nick aligned the pole with the slot. "It can be cozy."

"You've camped in the winter?"

Nick flashed her a grin. "Cupid loves sleeping in the snow."

Holly gave Cupid a side-eyed glance. "You would."

"Well, you'll just have to face it, Holly. You're a country girl now. And lucky for you, I can help you adjust. Starting with setting up our shelter for the night."

Holly smirked. "At least I've got a cute teacher."

"And I've got the prettiest teacher's assistant in the world."

They smiled at each other as they continued their work. Though Nick, ever the experienced outdoorsman, guided Holly through the process with patient instructions on erecting their shelter for the night, she fumbled with the fabric, tangled the rods, and tied knots in all the wrong places. All the while, her legs were still protesting from the long hike up the mountain.

She carefully positioned one of the final tent poles, attempting to align it with the designated slot, eager to prove her worth in this collaborative endeavor. Her hand slipped, and she was punished by the hot sting of friction on her cut. That momentary lapse in focus caused the post to slip from her fingers. One second, the pole stood vertical; the next, it succumbed to gravity. Aluminum collided with a resounding *thud* against Nick's unsuspecting head, jarring the serene atmosphere of their campsite.

Holly's gasp was quickly followed by a curse. Her hands flew to her cheeks. The rod clattered to the ground, an echo of her embarrassment reverberating through the air.

Nick winced, his narrow gaze shifting from the fallen pole to Holly. His rugged features twisted from momentary pain to amusement. He rubbed his head, a smile playing at the corners of his lips. "I have the feeling you resent me bringing you here."

Holly hurried to his side, kneeling beside him and cradling his head. "I'm so sorry, Nick. I didn't mean … Are you all right? Oh, God, maybe this was a mistake."

Nick chuckled, turning so they were face to face, the canvas resting on their heads. "No. It's not a mistake, Holly. It's going to be totally worth it. Believe me."

Chapter Two

From the inside of their fully erected canvas shelter, Cupid stretched a paw toward Holly and let out a short whimper.

Holly's brow lifted. "I don't know what you're complaining about. I'm the one freezing while you're wearing a fur coat."

Cupid tilted his head, and his tongue bounced as he panted.

"Come on." Now dressed in the outfit she planned for day two, Holly smoothed out the sleeping bag and stood. The top of her head didn't quite reach the tent's ceiling, but Nick would have to hunch over. "Let's see if he's got that fire started."

Cupid whipped through the flap, darting out ahead of Holly. The icy breeze pricked at her cheeks as she emerged. *Good thing I packed those extra layers.*

With the darkening heavens, nearby frogs and crickets sang their evening songs.

Nick crouched over the firepit and peeked at her over his shoulder. The sides of his mouth tugged upward as he stood. He briskly rubbed his palms together, his nose rosy.

"Are you sure it's August?" Holly pulled the zipper of her jacket higher. "Shouldn't it be toasty warm or something?"

Nick closed the distance between them and placed a hand on the small of her back. "If it's warmth you're looking for, I think I can help."

She flashed him a coy smile. "I'm going to hold you to that."

"Aha. My plan worked."

As Nick leaned in for a kiss, the fire he'd started released a loud crackle. Cupid jumped back and barked at the flames.

"How's your head?" Holly stretched to give the spot that got whacked by the pole a gentle stroke.

"It's fine. I'm just glad the poles aren't steel." He reached for her hand. "How's your cut?"

"I barely noticed it until now. The cold air helps." She entwined her fingers with his.

"Good. Now that we've survived our injuries, we can concentrate on this glorious fire I created with my bare hands."

Holly chuckled at Nick's over-the-top muscleman poses. "Quit it. Please." She grabbed his biceps. "You've already won me over with your prowess as an outdoorsman."

Nick adopted a caveman dialect. "But fire big. Scary. Impressive."

"Yes. Impressive." Holly roped her arms around his waist and set her head on his arm. "And romantic."

His warm breath caressed her forehead as he leaned in and kissed her temple.

Campfire smoke wafted up into the night sky. The flames cast dancing shadows across Nick's face, playing with the scruff on his jawline. Holly flattened out her insulated mat and sat, a chill of excitement bubbling through her.

"Have you seen them before?" she asked. "The Northern Lights?"

"Yeah, once when I was a kid. My mom and dad brought me and Rachel out here. Rachel was in a bad mood at the beginning of the trip because she didn't want to be away from her friends. I remember my mom being so patient with her, just letting Rachel's complaints roll off her back. And then the lights appeared, and Rachel couldn't stop talking about them. My mom had this knowing smirk, and I felt then that she was the smartest woman in the universe."

WEDDING BELLS IN SILVERWOOD

"Sounds like she was very wise."

"Rachel wanted to come up here every year after that, but it didn't quite work out."

Holly put a hand on his. "Is that when your mom got sick?"

Nick bit his lip and nodded.

She stared at their joined hands. Her heart swelled, feeling even closer to Nick. One of the things that they'd had in common and bonded over was losing a parent—Holly's father and Nick's mother.

A cool breeze swept through, and Holly shivered. Nick wrapped an arm around her, and she breathed in the woodsy scent of his cologne.

Holly nuzzled into him. "Well, I've never really been the outdoorsy, sleep-under-the-stars type, but maybe that's just because I didn't have the right camping partner."

"It does improve the experience altogether."

When she shivered this time, it wasn't from the chilly wind but Nick's intense gaze.

"Hey." He raised his brows. "I've got marshmallows."

"Now you're speaking my language."

Nick retrieved the packet and extendable roasting sticks while the hot chocolate was warming on the grate above the fire. To keep the bag from being swept up by the cold wind, Nick set a rock on it. He slid a marshmallow on each of his and Holly's sticks and handed one to her.

"I haven't done this since I was a kid." Holly held out her stick, hovering her sugary treat over the flames. Nick's marshmallow was soon beside hers.

"All we're missing now are some spooky stories." Nick waggled his brows.

"If you want to hear some scary stories, I can tell you more about when I lived in New York."

"It couldn't have been that bad."

Holly snickered. "No, it wasn't. New York is lovely, but I'm much happier in Silverwood. With you." Holly had moved to Silverwood to escape the constant reminder of her failed art career. The mountain cabin she'd inherited from her father provided the perfect retreat, but once she fell in love with the quaint town—and the incredible man by her side—she couldn't imagine living elsewhere.

Holly rotated her stick but a little too fast. Her marshmallow was there one second, and then the next, it had disappeared into the pit. At first, she could only stare at the melting sugar. With everything that had gone wrong during the day, losing the marshmallow somehow didn't surprise her. She let out a small laugh. "Seriously?"

When she turned to face Nick, laughter erupted from his throat. The joyous sound echoed in chorus with the crackling flames. Holly couldn't help but be infected by his mirth, her giggles bubbling forth as they shared the lighthearted moment. Eventually, their laughs subsided, leaving behind a lingering warmth and a sense of quiet contentment in the tranquility of the night.

The fire popped and crackled, embers dancing midair as the flames brightened.

Nick checked his watch and then bent his head back to look at the sky. "Now, if Mother Nature would play nice, we might get a glimpse of what we came here to see."

Holly shifted to rest her head on his shoulder. She pressed her lips together, steadfastly refusing to let the frigid temperature dampen the romantic vibe by setting her teeth to a cacophony of chattering. Though the appearance of the Northern Lights seemed to take some time, she didn't mind. She was content to wait in the comfort and warmth of Nick's arms.

And then the energy in the air changed, and the color of the heavens transformed. Holly stood, and Nick followed suit.

Bright lights danced above her eyes, forming a delightful curtain of sparkling colors. She swore she could hear a slight hum in the atmosphere. Magic was literally in the air. Holly sensed something special was about to happen. The exciting feeling of anticipation made her heart race.

"It's so fascinating. I don't understand it, but I love it."

"Well, it's caused by activity on the sun's surface. Solar storms charge particles with electricity at the Earth's poles, and—" Nick laughed. "Oh. You weren't really looking for an explanation, were you?"

She smiled as she leaned into him. "Not really. But you sure are cute explaining stuff."

His gaze softened, and he released a shuddered breath before pulling her closer. "Holly, I have something to confess."

"Oh?"

He bit his lip, his eyes cast downward.

Holly leaned away to see him better. "Nick?"

"I had an ulterior motive for bringing you here."

She searched his face. "Wh-what motive?"

His lips quivered. *Trembled* was more like it. Holly's heartbeat quickened. Nick could hear it, she was certain.

He ran his thumb along her jaw. "Holly."

"You're making me shiver." It wasn't from the cold. She hardly noticed her frozen fingers and toes anymore.

"I'm sorry." He let out a small chuckle and shook his head. "It's just that I've been going over the right way to do this in my head. The most meaningful and memorable way. If a man's lucky, he'll only do this once in his life."

"Do …?" Holly swallowed hard. Was she even breathing?

"Starting with the magic of the Northern Lights tonight, I

promise to fill each of your days with as much magic as I can if you allow me." He searched her face as he shifted, bending until he balanced on one knee.

When he dug into his coat pocket, Holly covered her mouth. The world seemed to spin, the sparkling colors of the aurora borealis glimmering in her periphery as Nick presented an open, black velvet box. The diamond ring nestled in the satin interior reflected the prism shimmering above their heads.

"Holly, I feel connected to you in a way I've never felt to anyone. I can't imagine spending a single day of my life without you in it. The day your car skidded into that ditch was a blessing because it was the catalyst that brought you to me, and you skidded into my heart."

She laughed as tears trickled down her cheeks.

"Every day I am in your presence, I find a thousand more things I love about you. And I could spend my life doing that if you let me. Will you do me the honor of marrying me?"

Nick looked at Holly, seemingly holding his breath as he awaited her answer. Meanwhile, Cupid jumped up on his hind legs, his front paws bent as if he were begging.

She had to inhale to get her voice to work. Nodding, she lowered her hands. "Yes. Yes, I will."

His smile was almost as bright as the colored beams surrounding them. Standing, he took her hand and slipped the ring onto her finger.

"Oh, Nick!" She threw her arms around him as their lips met. As the kiss deepened, the buzzing of the aurora borealis became a choir of angels singing their approval. If someone told her a few years ago that she could feel this happy, this blessed, she might have said they were crazy. But now, with Nick embracing her under the magical sky, she knew their love was meant to be.

Chapter Three

Holly could barely contain her excitement, bouncing on her toes as she scanned the crowd of departing passengers. Her anticipation had Cupid pacing back and forth in front of her and Nick. It had been over two years since she'd seen her mother. When Holly's aunt Lita had been diagnosed with Type 2 diabetes, Holly's mom decided to return to the Philippines to care for her. This was the longest Holly had gone without a visit, and her wedding—combined with the holidays—served as the perfect occasion for the mother-daughter reunion.

Nick placed a hand on the small of Holly's back. "Maybe you shouldn't have had that second cup of coffee."

"I don't think it would have mattered." Holly pointed. "Oh, there she is." She stepped forward and waved.

Vivian St. Ives, all four-foot-ten of her, rolled her suitcases toward them. She stopped once to wave, copying how Holly bounced on her heels, before continuing, taking quick steps with her short legs. Even with a huge smile, her face contained barely any wrinkles. She beamed at Holly and Nick with big, brown eyes. Though her dark hair was thinner than Holly remembered, it was still long enough to be twisted into a messy bun.

"Holly, my baby girl." Despite living in the States for many years, Vivian still had a strong, endearing Filipino accent.

Holly rushed into her mother's open arms. "Mom, it's so good to see you."

As her mom backed out of the embrace, she took Holly's face in her hands. "You look great. Younger, even. This mountain air is doing you good." Her gaze went to Nick. "Or maybe it's love."

"Hello, Mrs. St. Ives." Nick bent down to hug her. "It's nice to finally meet you in person."

"Call me Vivi," she insisted. As she withdrew, her heels came down to touch the floor. "Oh, you're much taller than I expected. Video chats don't really do people justice."

Cupid whined, clearly confused by all the hugging.

"Wow," Vivian exclaimed. "He's even more beautiful than on the computer."

"He is a looker," Nick agreed.

Vivian crouched down and ran her fingers through Cupid's fur. "And so *fluffy*."

Cupid sniffed Vivian's face and licked her cheek.

Vivian giggled. "That settles it. You're sleeping in my bed. Then I won't need such a thick blanket."

"Come on, Mom. There'll be plenty of time later for puppy kisses." Holly took the handle of one of her mother's suitcases. "Let's get you to the cabin."

"Yes. I've been dying to see it after all this time."

Nick took the other suitcase and led them to the parking garage.

It wasn't until they were on the road and heading toward town that Holly could catch her breath.

"My goodness." Vivian stared out the side window, a wide smile on her face, taking in the view of the surrounding mountains. "I feel like it's been forever since I've seen snow. I forgot how gorgeous Silverwood is."

Holly grinned, reveling in the excitement in her mother's voice. She always found her upbeat mannerisms and positive attitude infectious, and being around her excitability was one of the things she missed most.

"Is there anything special you want to see while you're here? I mean, aside from our wedding." Holly reached over and settled a hand on Nick's arm as he drove. She still couldn't wrap her head around the fact they were getting married in three weeks.

"Well, the wedding is the main event, isn't it? Other than that, not much." Vivian leaned forward between Nick's and Holly's seats. "But I do want to have a bite at The Gingerbread House and take a look at the art school. And, of course, I can't wait to go to Silverwood's famous Christmas Market."

Holly laughed and exchanged a look with Nick. "Not much, huh?"

"How is the school, by the way?" Vivian asked.

"It's been going really well." Delight surged through her. "Emily—Mrs. Weedleman—pops in now and then to see how we're doing, and I get to work with Lucy every day, which is amazing."

Vivian clapped her hands. "Tell me how Lucy is. I can't believe someone I knew as a little girl has a baby now."

Holly smiled at the thought of her long-time friend. "Lucy is good. You'll get to see her—and Samantha Grace."

"Such a lovely name. Sounds like a princess."

"She can be." Holly shook her head. "She's almost one and as stubborn as her mother."

"Time sure does fly." Vivian placed a hand on Holly's shoulder. "I can still remember when you were one."

Nick glanced at Vivian in the rearview mirror. "I bet she was a handful."

Vivian chuckled. "You've got that right."

Vivian went silent when Nick flipped the indicator to turn onto the next street. Holly twisted to face her and found her mother's eyes welling up.

Holly's brows shot upward. "Mom, are you okay?"

Vivian worried her lip for a moment. "It's our street."

"Yeah."

"Well …" Vivian swallowed. "I haven't been to the cabin since before your father died."

Holly's throat felt thick with tears, and her chest tightened. She reached back, comforted when her mother took her hand.

"Are you going to be okay with this?" Holly asked.

"Yes. Yes, of course. I can practically hear your father saying, 'It's about time you went to the cabin. What took you so long?' He always said Christmas wasn't the same if we weren't spending it in Silverwood."

When the house came into view, Vivian let out a soft "Oh."

Pure, white snow surrounded the picket fence. A picturesque, one-story cabin was nestled within the place Holly called home. Not just now but for all her childhood holidays. The home Holly's father had left her in his will.

Nick had barely parked the car before Vivian stepped onto the driveway. She stood there, staring at the structure, until Holly came to her side. Vivian sighed and took Holly's hand.

Cupid bounded out of the car and sniffed around in the snow before sauntering to the front door, wagging his tail.

"Ready to go in?" Holly asked her mother.

"Yes." Vivian beamed. "Let's."

Nick followed them to the porch while Holly fished the key out of her purse. Once they strode inside, everyone paused in the entranceway.

Vivian's eyes were glassy as she gazed over the space. Holly couldn't be sure, but she could swear her mom was holding her breath. Perhaps it was her way of stopping time to fully absorb her return to the cabin. Vivian released a slow sigh and made her way deeper into the house. Nick and Holly exchanged a look as they waited for Vivian to say something.

"This place belonged to his parents." With a small smile, Vivian ran her hand along the fireplace mantle. "He helped his father—your grandfather—redo the floors. I think that's where his love of carpentry stemmed from."

Vivian let out a laugh, seeming lost in memories. "I can remember when we first brought you here, Holly. You'd just started walking, and your father was paranoid that you'd somehow get hurt. He went to a lot of trouble babyproofing every room. He did everything to keep you safe, and after all that, he had the sense of humor to accuse me of being overprotective."

Though a pang of sorrow squeezed at her heart, Holly gave her mother a soft smile.

Vivian turned to Nick. "Holly learned to paint here, you know?"

"Is that right?" Nick prompted.

"Her father was repainting some furniture, and when he wasn't looking, little five-year-old Holly picked up his paintbrush and gave everything in sight a fresh coat of white paint."

A blush warmed Holly's cheeks.

Vivian chuckled. "But instead of getting mad, my Jake saw the sparkle in her eyes and bought her some fingerpaints and a big block of paper. She spent hours with those paints. We went through them in two days and had to get her more."

Holly gave her a sideways smile. "I'd like to think I've blossomed artistically since then."

Vivian laid a hand on Holly's arm. "You sure have."

"I agree." Nick crossed his arms and lifted his chin.

Vivian made her way over to the seven-foot tree in the living room, decorated with ornaments she and Holly's father had bought when they were newlyweds.

"Jake always loved a good Christmas tree." Vivian gently caressed one of the branches. "And this tree is gorgeous."

Holly touched Nick's arm. "Nick picked it out for you."

"Oh, that's right." Vivian turned to Nick. "You work on a tree farm."

"He owns it, Mom." Holly looked between her mom and Nick.

Nick wrapped his arm around Holly's waist, waggling his brows once. "She's right, though. I work on it, too."

Vivian winked. "I like him. He's clever."

"Mom, you should come take a look at the sleigh." Holly indicated toward the garage with her head.

"Yes, let's take a look." Vivian straightened her blouse. "Tell me again how your father saved the Christmas festival tree decorating contest."

Though they shared the story many times over video calls, Nick began telling it again. "We entered the state tree decorating contest to win the grand prize."

"Nick's father needed the money to cover the treatment of his Wilson's disease," Holly added.

"That's the copper buildup in the body, right?" Vivian asked.

"Yeah." Holly gestured for her mother to follow as she made her way to the door that led to the garage. "The whole town was in on it."

"But the night before the judges arrived," Nick continued, "a storm knocked down the beautiful, fully decorated, twenty-five-foot Christmas tree right into one of the festival stands."

"It caught fire." Holly opened the connecting door. "But Nick extinguished it."

Vivian and Nick entered the garage, and Holly and Cupid followed.

"So we needed a new tree," Nick went on.

"We drove through the dangerous storm to Nick's farm," Holly said.

"And we got a new tree. But my truck got stuck in the snow."

"There was no cell reception." Holly waved her hands back and forth.

Nick shook his head. "We were in a pickle."

"But Dad's sleigh was in the back of his truck." Holly gestured at the tarped form in front of them.

"It was big enough to transport the new tree in the snow." Nick stuffed his fists in his pockets. "All that was missing was a team of dogs to pull it."

Holly smiled. "So I got Cupid to howl to call his siblings to come to the rescue."

Vivian chuckled. "And there were nine of them, all named after the reindeer from the song?"

"Yep," Holly answered.

Vivian clapped her hands together once. "That's incredible."

"And they saved the day." Nick snaked an arm around Holly.

"And we won the contest." Holly looked up at Nick with a grin.

Cupid barked as if wanting to add to the story.

Vivian patted Nick's shoulder. "Your father's a lucky man to have people in his life who love him so much."

"He is, indeed." Nick beamed.

"Well?" Vivian nudged him with her elbow. "Let's see it."

Nick pulled the tarp off the giant form in the middle of the garage, unveiling the handcrafted sleigh Jake St. Ives had spent years mastering.

Vivian's hands flew to her face, and she pressed her palms against her cheeks. "It's even more beautiful than I remember." She ran her fingers along the side and patted the thick, red cushion—spacious enough for two adults—on the front bench. "It's bigger than I recall, too."

Cupid moved beside her, sniffing the sleigh.

Holly admired the perfectly sanded curves and polished rails.

Vivian faced her, tears pricking her eyes. "Your father loved working on this." She stopped as her voice caught in her throat.

Holly placed an arm around her mother's shoulders and squeezed.

Vivian's smile turned into a lengthy yawn. She tried to stifle it with her hand, but there was no stopping it.

"Oh, Mom. You're exhausted. It's the middle of the night in the Philippines. You must be all mixed up."

"It's just a bit of jetlag. I've survived worse than missing a bit of beauty sleep."

Holly shook her head. "Why don't you lie down? We can catch up more after you've rested."

Vivian waved her concerns away with an exaggerated flick of her hand. "That reminds me, Holly, dear. I have something for you."

"That's sweet, Mom, but I think it should wait until after you deal with your sleep deprivation. I've fixed up my old room for you. I hope that's okay."

"Okay, okay. Fine." Vivian rolled her eyes, but a smile tugged at the corners of her lips anyway.

"I wish you a nice rest." Nick held open the door that led back inside. "We can take you to The Gingerbread House tomorrow if you'd like."

"I'd love that."

Chapter Four

Viola's mind wandered as she cleared tables at Nick's bakery-slash-lunch bistro. As usual during Christmas, The Gingerbread House was bustling with business. But Viola's shift was almost over, and she was trying to recollect the list of groceries she'd promised to pick up for her mother after she clocked out for the day. If only she had remembered to bring the actual paper she'd written the items on …

Suddenly, the tray flew from her hand, and Viola's thoughts scattered as plates and mugs crashed onto the floor.

She gaped in horror at the customer standing beside her, the man's beige coat stained with hot chocolate. The man pressed a finger to the Bluetooth device in his ear, his other hand frozen in the air near her arm, and his jaw hung agape.

"I'm so sorry." Viola wasn't sure if she should tend to the broken dishes or get something to soak up the dark mess from the man's expensive-looking apparel. Was it cashmere?

Just my luck.

"Hold on, Scott," the tall man with sun-kissed caramel-colored hair said into his device. "I just got attacked by a waitress. I'll call you back."

Viola blinked. "*Attacked?* No. I'm sorry, but you're the one who knocked my tray out of my hand. What were you doing standing behind me anyway?"

"I wasn't standing behind you. I was reaching for my briefcase."

The man pointed to a leather attaché sitting under the adjacent table. "You backed into me. And ruined my coat. I will look ridiculous showing up to my meeting like this."

"I'm sorry about your coat, but you surely can't place all the blame on me."

He pressed his lips into a hard line and narrowed his eyes. "Whatever happened to 'the customer is always right'?"

Viola felt everyone in the shop staring at her. "I think the word *always* is a smidge extreme. And outdated. How about 'the customer is usually right unless he's being a condescending jerk'?"

His brows lifted. Viola swore one corner of his mouth twitched. Did he think this was funny?

A figure appeared from the other side of the counter. As Nick strolled toward them, Viola swept a strand of brunette hair that had escaped her ponytail behind her ear.

"Hi, I'm Nick. The owner." He extended his hand. "Looks like there's been a misunderstanding here."

The man shook Nick's hand. "Jonas Brickman. And yes. Someone here clearly has problems understanding."

Viola almost gasped when Jonas looked at her.

Nick subtly released a measured exhale. He placed a hand on Viola's shoulder and gave her the smallest of smiles.

"Viola, your shift's over, right? Why don't you go ahead and clock out? I'll deal with this mess." He faced Jonas. "I apologize for all of this. Let me take care of the bill for you, and if you need to be reimbursed for dry cleaning, just let me know."

Jonas nodded. Viola had to turn away to avoid the cocky grin on his face.

"Thanks, Nick." Viola chewed her lip to avoid saying anything more as she stomped to the back room.

Viola's face grew hot, and her lip was sore from biting it.

Frustration burned in her veins. She gathered her cobalt blue peacoat and white scarf in the back, then closed her eyes and blew out a slow breath. She had to calm down. It wasn't the first time she'd dealt with a difficult customer. Although, difficult customers were few and far between in Silverwood. Still, something about that man—*Jonas Brickman*—got under her skin.

Viola peeked through the doorway to see if the coast was clear. Upon seeing no trace of the arrogant man, she walked toward the door, sparing only a second to wave goodbye to Nick.

She headed for her car almost robotically. Somehow, she arrived at the store parking lot without remembering the drive. Try as she might, she couldn't turn off her inner dialogue about the encounter with Jonas.

Cut it out. He's not worth it.

Viola grabbed a handheld shopping basket and waved at the manager of Silverwood Grocery as she beelined for the vegetable aisle of the shop. It wasn't that there was no time for pleasantries; she simply had to calm herself before inadvertently letting her anger out on some unsuspecting soul.

Why was she still replaying the shouting match in her head?

Okay, 'shouting match' is a bit of an exaggeration. But he was *rude.*

Who did this Jonas Brickman think he was anyway? If there was one thing Viola detested, it was someone who considered themselves superior. Judging by his coat and suit, Jonas Brickman was probably a wealthy businessman who enjoyed reminding others of how important he was.

She snatched a bundle of carrots and practically threw them into her basket. *How dare he insult my intelligence? He doesn't even know me.*

She had to stop herself as she realized she was crushing an eggplant. Clearing her throat, she set the eggplant in her basket and exhaled slowly.

Viola forced herself to think of something else, mumbling a curse each time her mind circled back. She was certain he thought he could get away with anything—including disregarding human decency—just because he was rich and handsome.

Whoa. Handsome? Where did that thought come from?

As she checked out, she put on a small smile for the woman at the register.

"Paper or plastic?" the cashier asked.

"No, thanks. I have my own." Viola, an environmentalist at heart, whipped out two cloth tote bags from her backpack and packed her groceries.

Viola adjusted the straps of her shopping bags, kicking the intrusive thoughts of Jonas Brickman to the curb. Her thoughts wandered to the presents she wanted to send to her sister while striding toward her car until a sharp bark sounded.

She froze. Less than a foot in front of her, a car was backing out—one she hadn't seen because of the large van beside it. Her muscles tensed, and she swallowed hard. If that bark hadn't stopped her, she would have been hit.

Still standing in place, she waited until the driver noticed her, which he did with an embarrassed wave before continuing on his way.

Viola sighed and glanced to her right, then smiled at the sable and white, wolf-like Alaskan Malamute, who sat patiently as its owner loaded her vehicle. Viola wasn't sure which of Cupid's siblings this was, but she needed to thank it with a friendly pat.

"Oh, hello." The woman—the local florist, Viola realized—placed a final bag inside the hatch before shutting her trunk.

"Is it okay if I pet your dog?" Viola asked. "I think he just saved my life."

"Is that a fact?"

"Yeah. That car that just left would have clipped me if he hadn't barked."

"Sounds about right. Blitzen has some quick reflexes. Sure, feel free to pet him. He would love that."

Viola bent forward and rubbed the top of Blitzen's head, whispering her gratitude. Blitzen panted, and Viola could have sworn his lips were forming a grin.

"You work with Nick, right?" the woman asked.

"Yes. I'm Viola."

"Oh, yeah. Evelyn Carver's daughter. I'm Melissa. Nice to meet you."

"Nice to meet you, too."

"And I'm glad Blitzen could be of service."

Viola gave her a nod. "Me too. I'll see you around."

Viola made a mental note to get flowers from Melissa's shop or a nice Christmas wreath or poinsettia for her mom.

Fifteen minutes later, Viola pulled into her mother's driveway, which she was relieved to see had been cleared of snow. Oliver had been by—the college student who helped her mother out with heavy lifting and other chores for extra cash.

Viola exited the car and glanced at her mother's quaint, two-story home. She couldn't help but recall running around the yard with her sister Sina when they were little, being pushed on the tire swing her father had hung from the big oak tree out front. And the nights she and Sina would refuse to come down from their treehouse after their mother had called them to dinner.

A tall, burly man with dirty blond hair sticking out from a black beanie climbed down a ladder propped against the garage. He set down the bag in his hand and waved.

"Oliver, I didn't think you'd still be here."

Oliver removed his gloves. "Your mom was worried the rain

gutters might be jammed."

"Didn't you clean them out in October?"

"Yeah, but she said Silverwood's due for more storms soon."

"Isn't it always?" She went to the trunk to retrieve her grocery bags. "Are you staying for dinner or working at the restaurant tonight?"

"No, I promised Amy we could catch a movie."

"Nice." Viola always thought Oliver and Amy made a perfect match.

"You need a hand with those before I take off?" he asked.

"No, thanks. I'm all set. Have fun at the movies. Say hi to Amy for me."

"Thanks. I will."

The sun was already setting on an otherwise bright and clear day. One more reason not to waste any more time dwelling on Jonas. The hinges on the door gave off their familiar squeaks as she carried the groceries into the house, and Viola made a note to add oiling them to Oliver's to-do list.

"Mom? It's me."

"Be right there." Her mother's voice came from another room.

The low, buzzing *whoosh* of Evelyn Carver's wheelchair grew louder as she moved closer to the kitchen. Viola unpacked the groceries, grouping the vegetables on the counter.

"Hi, sweetheart. You're a doll for picking those up for me." Evelyn wheeled nearer and grabbed the bundle of carrots to inspect. She lowered her glasses, which were nestled in her salt-and-pepper gray hair. As she rotated the vegetables in her hand, her delicate frame seemed to reflect the challenges she had weathered over the years. "How was your day?"

"It was fine. Nothing special." *Nothing worth mentioning, anyway.* "How was yours? I see Oliver shoveled the driveway."

"He's such a dear. He also dug out my mom's old recipe book for me."

"Oh, yeah? Were you thinking of making one of Grandma's recipes?"

Her mother flashed her a toothy grin. "Hence the spontaneous need for groceries. I was in the mood for her veggie casserole. And don't tell me I could just look one up on my phone. No one made that dish quite like your grandma."

Viola chuckled. "That's so true. I remember her letting me help her cook as a kid. I had to stand on a chair so I could reach the counter."

"That's right. It was always you and never Sina."

Viola raised an eyebrow. "Sina was more interested in selling the recipe. She's always had profit margins on her mind." She shuffled through the cards in the box. "Which of her veggie casseroles did you want to do? She has two versions."

"Hmm. Let's go with the milder one. I think the other calls for hot pepper flakes."

"I love that one, too. But sure." Viola shrugged. "We'll keep it on the mild side tonight."

Evelyn retrieved the cutting board while Viola washed the vegetables. It wasn't long before the kitchen was filled with delicious scents of rosemary and garlic and the sounds of delightful conversation and laughter.

The dish turned out better than Viola could have imagined. She liked to think the spirit of her grandmother had guided her hand through the process.

"Have you heard from your sister?" Evelyn asked as they settled down in the living room. "I wish she was coming home for Christmas."

"Me too." Viola threw a thick, crocheted blanket over her legs as she got cozy on the couch. "Sina texted me this morning. She's got so many projects to do for business school, but she promised to be home the week after New Year's."

Evelyn nodded. "Well, that's something, at least. Can't wait to have both my girls with me."

Viola stared at the twinkling lights on her mother's Christmas tree. It had been a long and stressful day, with one particular encounter she would rather forget.

She glanced back at her mother and found her head bent forward. A small snore escaped Evelyn's throat.

Viola pushed herself off the couch and unlocked the wheelchair's brake. Taking hold of its push handles, she gently drove her mother to her bedroom. Evelyn stirred with a soft moan.

"It's okay, Mom," Viola whispered. "I'll get you into bed."

"But the kitchen—"

"I'll take care of it. You get some sleep."

After tucking her mom in and checking that she had water near her bed, Viola cleared the kitchen and ran the dishwasher. Once the kitchen light was flipped off, she took the box of recipes, carried it to the living room, and made herself comfortable, her favorite throw pillow on her lap. She placed the box beside her and opened the lid. Faded, cream-colored recipe cards were stacked to the brim.

Viola's lips spread into a smile as she read the cards for chicken cordon bleu, roast duck, shrimp scampi, and more. Each dish transported her back to her childhood, to a simpler time. Elizabeth Winston had been the wisest, most loving person in the world. It was her grandmother who had first told Viola that she'd make a great chef one day.

Ever since she could remember, Viola had been passionate about working with food and creating dishes that brought smiles to people's faces. After her grandmother had passed away, Viola continued to cook, both because of her love for it and also as a way to keep her grandmother's memory alive. When she had gotten accepted to culinary school, she'd been ecstatic. She'd believed her dreams were at long last coming true. Culinary school had been harder than she'd expected, but Viola had worked her butt off perfecting her creations, learning the difference between a hollandaise and béarnaise sauce, how to make a *bouquet garni*, how to quarter and truss a chicken, and a million other methods and techniques the big-name chefs used. She'd had to write a paper presenting a business plan for a restaurant and a catering company and had received top marks for her structured and efficient concepts.

Things had been progressing according to her ideal timeline until her mother's car accident. The icy mountain roads had landed Evelyn Carver in the hospital, unable to walk. Viola and her sister had dropped everything to take care of their mother. After a few months, when Mrs. Carver had been doing better, Sina announced she was returning to business school in Missoula. Viola had felt obligated to stay in Silverwood and look after their mother, putting her dreams on hold.

But as much as she believed there was a missing piece of her life's journey she had to wait to fulfill, Viola didn't regret staying. She'd even go as far as to say the experience had brought them closer together. Deep down, however, she still held on to the hope that one day her aspirations would become reality. For now, waitressing would have to do.

The thought of her day job shoved the encounter with Jonas to the forefront of her mind again. *Did he have to be so rude? I hate men who don't take women seriously.*

She closed the recipe box and pressed the pillow against her face to stop herself from screaming.

Chapter Five

Silverwood's town square was the very definition of Christmas. As far as the eye could see, pine garlands were draped across every available surface, lights twinkled, and ornaments of every kind shone. The buzz of activity ahead of the festival was something to behold. Holly, Nick, and Vivian watched as little stands and huts were erected while festive music drifted through the air. Holly smiled at her mother, who was clearly dazzled by the festivities.

"You ready, Mom?"

Vivian patted Holly's arm. "Sure. Sure. Let's go."

Holly rubbed her hands together as the trio approached The Gingerbread House, their boots crunching on the light snow-covered sidewalk. Behind the paneled windows, a variety of Christmas-themed cupcakes greeted them. The quaint shop was filled with patrons, from customers taking pleasure in a simple cup of hot chocolate to hungry souls delving into the day's lunch special, every one of them enjoying themselves.

"Does it look like you remember it, Mom?" Holly lifted her brows and watched her mother's face.

"Oh, yes. Your father loved this eatery. He was particularly fond of the Bison Fudge." Vivian turned to Nick. "Do you still make that?"

"Absolutely." Nick propped the door open for his companions. "I can whip you up one right now if you'd like."

"That sounds wonderful." Vivian hooked her arm through

Holly's. "You'll share it with me, right? I could never finish the dish on my own—something your father always counted on."

As soon as they strode into the place, they were greeted by Viola, who'd appeared from behind the counter. Though Viola was cheerful, Holly could swear something was troubling her.

"Hey, Nick. Holly." Viola wiped her hands on her apron. "Need a table?"

"If there's one available," Nick replied.

"I just cleared one. Follow me." Viola led the way.

"This is my mom," Holly said as they removed their coats and hung them on the chair backs. "Vivian St. Ives."

"Nice to meet you." Viola handed her a menu.

"You, too, dear. And I already know what I want. I used to come here years ago and am dying to have an order of Bison Fudge."

"One of my favorites." Viola took the menu back and gave her a nod.

"Give her extra whipped cream," Nick said. "And I'll have a coffee. Black."

"A hot chocolate for me." Holly rubbed her palms together to warm them.

"You got it," Viola said. "I'll be back in a sec."

As Viola left to fulfill their orders, the three of them settled in their chairs.

"This is simply lovely," Vivian said, looking around and taking in the familiar surroundings.

"Vivian St. Ives?" The voice came from the entrance of the shop.

Holly recognized her baking-obsessed neighbor, Mrs. Miranelli, without having to turn.

"Janice." Vivian stood and smiled.

The robust, red-headed woman's faux fur coat added to her girth as she waddled toward them. "Vivian, when did you get into town?" Mrs. Miranelli embraced Holly's mother. When she released her, Mrs. Miranelli patted her ginger curls as if checking that they hadn't come undone. "I knew you had to be coming in for the wedding, but I didn't know when. And it's close to impossible to find either of these two busybodies to get the scoop." She gestured to Holly and Nick.

"I just arrived yesterday. I had plans to pop over and visit you as soon as I got settled." Vivian gave Mrs. Miranelli a friendly pat on her shoulder. "How's Henry?"

"Still the love of my life and a pain in the butt all rolled into one. So nothing's changed." Mrs. Miranelli chuckled heartily.

Viola reappeared, balancing a tray with their orders.

"Oh, this is us," Vivian announced. "We'll catch up later, okay?"

"It's a date." Mrs. Miranelli removed her scarf and shifted toward the counter. "I need to place my order before Henry files a missing person report."

Vivian sat at the table as Viola set down their drinks and fudge.

Holly put her hands around her mug to warm her fingers. "Dig in, Mom."

"Wow, this looks better than I remember." She picked up her fork and let it hover over the dessert, doing a little dance in her seat before slicing a bit of fudge and scooping some whipped cream with it. One taste and Vivian emitted a "Mmm."

"I take it it's good?" Nick asked.

"*Masarap*," Vivian replied. "That means delicious. Here, Holly, try some."

Holly was about to take the fork from her mom when her melodic ringtone interrupted her. "It's the caterer." She turned slightly away as she answered the call. "Hello?"

"Ms. St. Ives. This is Cheryl from Montgomery Catering."

"Yes, hello."

"I'm afraid I'm calling with bad news. It seems our partnership with Lakeside Chateau has unexpectedly and abruptly ceased. There is a lawsuit involved, and all business between the two parties has been henceforth discontinued. Unfortunately, that means that unless you move your wedding to another venue, we are unable to cater it and must terminate the contract."

Silence.

Is this a joke?

Holly couldn't wrap her head around the woman's words. "Wh-what? I don't understand."

"I'm sorry. Montgomery Catering is no longer permitted on Lakeside Chateau's premises because of the lawsuit. We apologize, but we have no choice. If you have another venue, we can still honor our contract. Otherwise, we have to bow out. We can send you back your deposit right away. Just let us know by the end of the week. And again, we apologize for the inconvenience."

"But the wedding is in three weeks." Holly stared at the phone, stunned that the woman had already hung up on her.

She felt as if her heart were lodged in her esophagus. How could this be happening? It had to be a joke. But who would play such a cruel prank? No. She had to face the facts—it was simply bad luck.

"Holly?" Nick leaned closer, searching her face. "What is it?"

"The caterer." Her throat was so dry that she could hardly get the words out. "They canceled."

"Canceled? What do you mean?" Holly's mother jumped to her feet, her napkin falling to the floor.

After delivering something to another table, Viola stopped to pick up the napkin.

"Did they say why?" Nick asked, his forehead wrinkled.

"Something about a lawsuit between them and the venue owner." Holly raked her fingers through her hair. It was as if all the air had left her lungs. "What are we going to do?"

Nick took Holly's hand in his. "Don't worry. We'll figure it out."

"They said if we booked another venue, they could still cater, but how are we supposed to do that on such short notice?" Holly looked up at Nick as if he'd surely have the answer.

"Did you have any other caterers in the running?" Viola set down her tray and placed her hands on her hips.

"They must be booked up by now." Holly felt as if she were going to hyperventilate.

"What's this I hear?" Mrs. Miranelli hurried over to them. "Your caterer dropped out?" She clicked her tongue. "I mean, that's awful. That's a real shame. And I hope you find a replacement. But, honey, I just wanted to say—and I don't mean to be too presumptuous—I would *love* to make your wedding cake."

"Oh, um, well …" Holly stood. *No, no, no. My guests will never forgive me for subjecting them to Mrs. Miranelli's baking.* She couldn't seem to get her mouth working properly to respond. She felt as if her eyes were bulging out of her head.

Nick shifted from one foot to the other, looking frazzled. He, too, knew the story of Holly's mad rush to the drugstore after Mrs. Miranelli's generous batch of tainted cookies.

Viola stepped forward, facing Mrs. Miranelli. "Actually, they've, uh, already asked me to do it."

Holly blanched and grabbed Nick's hand.

"You?" Mrs. Miranelli blinked, shaking her head at Viola. "When could they have possibly asked you? They just now got the cancellation."

Holly squeezed Nick's hand with both of hers. The situation seemed to be spiraling out of control, and she had no idea how to get a hold of it. Nick looked deeply into her eyes as if trying to convince her everything would be fine.

"They, uh, asked me to be the backup. Like, months ago." Viola visibly swallowed. "Because I went to culinary school. Now that the first caterer backed out, I'm catering the wedding."

"You are?" Holly could only stare at her, unsure of how she felt.

Viola widened her eyes for a second, her jaw clenched. It was apparent she was aiming to send Holly a signal. *I'm here to save you,* Viola's look seemed to relay.

"You *are*," Holly finally said. "Yes, um, right." She turned to Mrs. Miranelli. "Yeah, it totally slipped my mind that we asked Viola to be our backup. She, uh, went to culinary school."

Holly glanced at Nick, who nodded.

"Absolutely. She was at the top of her class." Nick patted Viola on the back. "We're lucky to have such a skilled chef catering our wedding. You've tasted her delicious pecan sticky cookies and her lemon bars. If you think about it, it all worked out for the best."

Mrs. Miranelli's eyes darted between them, her shoulders hunching slightly. "True, true. She does make an excellent lemon bar. Oh, all right. As long as you've got things squared away. But if you need any assistance, dear, I'm available."

Vivian placed a hand on Mrs. Miranelli's wrist. "That's so kind of you to offer, Janice. I'm certain these kids have got it all under control."

Mrs. Miranelli put on a smile so big Holly wondered if it was genuine. "Of course, you're right. They're all grown up, after all."

"So, Viola." Nick scratched the back of his neck. "Can we speak to you for a moment in the back?"

"Of course." Viola wrung her hands as she marched into the back room.

Holly whispered to her mother that they would be back shortly. Her heart was thumping so hard she believed everyone in the shop could hear it.

Once they were all out of earshot, Nick, Holly, and Viola spoke in hushed voices.

"What just happened?" Holly held the sides of her face.

"I don't know." Viola shook her head. "I panicked. It's like the words just flew out of my mouth."

"That's understandable." Nick paced the length of the small back room. "It was a good call not to allow Mrs. Miranelli to bake or cook anything for the wedding."

"Viola, can you really cater the event?" Holly asked. "I don't want to underestimate your skills, but I also don't want you to be overwhelmed."

Viola's eyes darted between Nick and Holly. Her breaths were shallow, and she was still wringing her hands. Holly and Nick kept silent as they waited.

"Definitely," Viola finally said. "I can do it. I've drawn up catering plans in culinary school. I worked a few jobs, and theoretically, I know what has to be done. I just have to find a crew to help in the kitchen and some catering waiters who can be available on New Year's Eve. Piece of cake, right?"

"Piece of wedding cake, if we're lucky." Nick snickered, but he sobered when the others kept straight faces. "Sorry."

"And as long as I can be more flexible with my hours here—" Viola began.

"Sure, of course." Nick waved a dismissive hand. "Anything you need, you've got it."

"Okay." Holly couldn't stop nodding. It was as if every nod would convince her more and more that it would all work out. "Okay. We can pull this off. Yes. Let's do it. We can give you the deposit when we get the refund from the first caterer."

"No, no. I can pay you upfront," Nick insisted. "I want you to be able to get everything you need sooner rather than later."

Viola visibly swallowed. "Great. Thank you."

"Thank *you*, Viola. We'll send you all the information you need. And you can come with me to the venue to get acquainted with the kitchen." Holly put a hand on Nick's arm. "We better get back to my mom before she thinks we eloped."

Chapter Six

Viola had only been to Lakeside Chateau for a birthday party as a kid. Everyone at that party had spent the entire afternoon ice skating. There would be no skating today, however. A good portion of the lake was blocked off with signs warning that the ice was too thin.

Viola followed Holly toward the massive building where the wedding and reception would occur. Somehow, the chateau appeared much bigger now, and Viola wondered if the owners had added a wing or two since her last visit. Snow covered the manicured hedges and shrubs, and the bare trees on the lawn were strewn with fairy lights.

Viola craned her neck to take in the steeply pitched gable roof, the multiple chimneys with decorative caps, and the balustraded terrace. She wondered how much Holly and Nick spent to have it as their wedding venue.

At the front center of the building was a wide, cream-colored marble stairway that led to a broad veranda with a wrought-iron railing. The expansive entryway was accentuated with ten-foot-tall, paned-glass double doors. Beside the doors stood an elegantly decorated Christmas tree. As they approached, one of the double doors opened, and a statuesque woman with flame-red hair greeted them with a smile.

"Hello, Ms. St. Ives." The woman shook Holly's hand before offering Viola a handshake. "You must be Ms. Carver. I'm Susan

Stettly. Please, come inside. I'll show you to the kitchen."

Viola felt as if she'd just been transported to a palace when they entered the building. The curved staircase in the entrance hall drew attention to the high ceilings, all lit by an elegant chandelier. Viola trailed after Holly but was distracted by the shiny marble floors, the stylish sconces adorning the walls, and the expensive-looking furniture.

Viola's hands tightened into fists as she blew out a long breath. The prospect of taking on the job already overwhelmed her, but now, seeing the enormity and sophistication of the building—no, *mansion*—it was hard not to feel small and in over her head.

Come on. Pull yourself together. You learned how to do this. Now's your chance to show your skills.

"Ms. St. Ives, I once again sincerely apologize for the inconvenience caused by our former catering partner," Susan said.

They followed her through an elaborate dining room. Round tables were adorned with pristine white tablecloths and tall crystal vases filled with pastel pink roses.

Susan glanced over her shoulder as they approached a set of swinging double doors. "I'm afraid the decision to part with them was unavoidable. The timing, of course, is extremely inconvenient. As a gesture of gratitude for understanding, we will grant you a ten percent discount on the venue's price. The establishment's owner is on the way to greet you and personally apologize for the hassle."

"That's very kind," Holly replied. "Thank you."

"This is the kitchen." Susan held one of the doors open so they could enter. "I hope it suits your needs, Ms. Carver."

Viola gaped at the immaculate kitchen, which measured roughly one thousand square feet and was filled with silver appliances. She counted five working areas, the most important being the cooking, washing, and storage sections. There was also a station of worktops for food preparation and doors that surely led to a pantry. Everything appeared brand new.

"Certainly." Viola nodded. "It looks perfect."

Susan pressed the folder she was carrying to her chest. "Well, it's all yours. At least until the first week of January, when the chateau hosts another event. Unfortunately for us, two other events that were to occur between now and then were canceled because of the caterer situation. They couldn't make it work."

"Oh, that's a shame," Viola said.

"Yes, it's a pity." Susan tilted her head. "But that means you've got the kitchen to yourself, so feel free to schedule your deliveries and invoices here."

"Wow." Viola cleared her throat, telling herself to act more professional. "I mean, thank you. I'll do that."

Susan smiled at her and then faced Holly again. "I've got the paperwork here to amend the catering event, so we can start filling that out while we wait for Mr. Brickman."

Viola stiffened, unable to catch her breath. She stared while Susan took papers out of the folder.

Brickman? What are the chances?

Holly signed the documents, and Susan closed the file.

"Mr. Brickman should be here shortly." Susan propped the folder in her arm. "I'll put this in its proper place, but if you need anything, you can find me in my office."

"You okay, Viola?" Holly asked once they were alone. "You've gone pale."

"Did she say Brickman?"

"Mm-hm, he's the owner. Relatively new, I guess. Took over a year ago, I think." Holly wrinkled her brow. "Why?"

It couldn't be the same guy. Could it?

Viola shook her head. She wasn't sure what to do with her hands other than clutch her notebook until her knuckles turned white. Her mouth was dry, and a muscle twitched near her eye.

Viola blew out a long breath at the sound of footsteps coming nearer in the hall. She wished her hands weren't so clammy. If the owner turned out to be someone other than Jonas, she didn't want to make a bad impression.

"A ten percent discount," Holly whispered. "At least that's something. I didn't want to lose this venue. The ceremony is taking place in the enclosed winter garden—the one that leads out to the lake. It has a beautiful view of the mountains. I fell in love with it as soon as I saw it. I can show it to you after we've spoken to Mr. Brickman."

"You know Mr. Brickman was at The Gingerbread House the other day?" Viola asked. "At least, I assume it was the same Mr. Brickman."

"He was?"

"But Nick didn't seem to know who he was when he introduced himself."

"Oh, yeah." Holly shook her head. "No, we haven't met him. We've always worked with Susan for everything."

"I see. That explains it, then." Now Viola felt even worse for ruining Jonas's coat.

The door swung open, and Viola's suspicions were confirmed. Jonas was typing something into his phone. The silver-gray suit he wore appeared to be freshly pressed. Viola's memory of how handsome he was hadn't lived up to the reality. Her heart skipped a beat. Was it because she was nervous? Or was it something else? Before Jonas lifted his head, Viola twisted away to catch her breath.

Jonas approached Holly, holding out his hand and flashing a confident smile. "Hello, Ms. St. Ives. It's great to meet you. Sorry it has to be under such unfavorable circumstances. And again, thank you for understanding the special situation we're in. I don't want to trouble you with the specifics of the lawsuit, but I'm glad to hear you could arrange for another caterer."

The pleasant scent of his cologne hit her nose. Viola breathed it in deeply, wishing she didn't enjoy it so much. Or at all. She turned to face him, forcing a polite expression.

Jonas's brow furrowed. "You?"

Viola's small smile disappeared. "Me."

Holly tilted her head. "Viola said you were at my fiancé's café the other day, but I get the feeling there's more to the story."

"Your fiancé's café?" Jonas asked.

"The Gingerbread House."

"Of course. Nick Mason. I didn't even put that together until now." Jonas scrubbed at his chin, his eyes fleetingly landing on Viola. "You'll have to excuse me. So much paperwork flies across my desk every day. I hardly have time to match up names and places."

An awkward silence hovered in the room.

Holly looked from Jonas to Viola. "Am I missing something?"

"No." Viola shook her head. "Nothing at all."

"I thought you were a waitress," Jonas said to Viola.

"I graduated at the top of my class in culinary school."

"But have you catered before?" He crossed his arms.

"I worked on a crew during my internship, yes."

He tapped his fingers against his arm. "Working on a crew and managing one are two totally different things. Do you have experience managing an event like this?"

His accusatory tone caused Viola to set her jaw. "Is there going to be a problem here?" Viola asked.

"Mr. Brickman," Holly said, interrupting. "My fiancé and I have complete faith that Viola can handle the job."

Viola was unsure if Holly's words boosted her confidence or

heightened her anxiety. She really didn't want to miss this opportunity.

Jonas's focus went between Holly and Viola for a moment. Then he smiled. "I see. I'm sorry to have doubted your judgment, Ms. St. Ives. And as I'm sure Susan has informed you, we would like to offer you a ten percent discount—"

Viola tuned out the rest of the discussion as the acid in her stomach swirled.

You can do this. Don't allow this guy to let you doubt yourself. You were top of your class.

Viola straightened her shoulders, aiming to be confident. If only she could convince herself that she could be.

Chapter Seven

Viola held her pen firmly, her phone pressed up against her ear. She was almost through her list of potential help for the catering event. So far, two of the twelve people she had called were available to work the wedding. All she needed now was at least one more person for the kitchen and a few waiters to serve. Her list included old friends from her school days in Silverwood, coworkers at The Gingerbread House, and people she knew who worked in the food service industry. The final handful of names at the bottom of her list were people who lived outside of Silverwood, and though she didn't have high hopes that any of them would be available, she was holding out for a miracle before New Year's Eve.

"So, yeah," Viola said into the phone. "I know it's last minute, James, and it's the holiday season, but is there any chance you might be able to spare a few hours to work the event?"

"You won't believe this," James began, "but I actually can help out. My folks went out west to visit my sister in California, so I'm family-obligation free."

"That's perfect. Thank you so much, James. I can text you the details."

"Works for me. It'll be great to see you again. I always knew you'd make it as a chef."

Viola winced. *This must be what imposter syndrome feels like.* "That's so nice of you to say. Thanks. I'll see you then."

"Bye."

She sighed as she set down the phone. Putting a checkmark next to James's name, she forced herself to invite the good feelings in and stop panicking.

It's working. I'm doing it. I just have to have faith in myself.

The sound of her mother's wheelchair caused her to turn.

"Hey, Mom."

"Hi, honey. Were you on the phone?"

"Yeah, I had some calls to make. I've got three people so far to help me with the catering job."

Evelyn intertwined her fingers and held them under her chin. "Oh, Viola, that's wonderful."

Viola cringed.

"What?" Evelyn leaned forward. "What's wrong?"

Viola stood and placed her hands behind her aching neck, stretching it out. "A couple of things, I guess."

"Honey, you can talk to me. What's bothering you?"

"Well, for one, I feel like I'm abandoning you."

Evelyn shook her head. "What? Viola, no. Why would you say that?"

"Because this wedding is going to take a lot of my time. I know Oliver can be here to help you out when I can't be here, but between working at The Gingerbread House and organizing the catering, I'll rarely be around at all. And I don't want to do that to you."

"Viola, come here." Evelyn rolled nearer to the table and patted the nearest chair.

Viola pressed her lips together and took a seat.

"You are not abandoning me." Evelyn took her hand. "If anything, I've kept you rooted to one spot for far too long."

"No, you di—"

"Yes. I'm not naïve. I know you had to put all your dreams on hold for me. I never meant to force you into that position."

Viola squeezed her hand. "No, Mom, of course not. I don't blame you. It's not your fault this happened to you."

"But it was also not your responsibility to cast everything aside to take care of me."

"I wanted to. And these last few years? I think it brought us even closer than we were before. I wouldn't have traded that time with you for the world."

"I'm glad we had all this time together, too." Evelyn sighed. "But now you've got an opportunity to jump into the thing you've been waiting to do since you were a little girl, and there's no way I'm going to stand in your way—no pun intended."

Though guilt and uncertainty threatened to crush her stomach, Viola felt her shoulder muscles loosen. "Thank you, Mom."

"As for the extra time you'll be working, don't worry. I can manage a lot on my own. And the stuff I can't? Well, that's what Oliver is for, right?"

"I'm sure he won't mind putting in extra hours if necessary."

"See." Evelyn tapped Viola's hand. "It's no problem at all."

"I guess."

Evelyn searched her face. "What's the other thing?"

"What?"

"You said a couple of things were bothering you."

"Oh. Yeah, that." Viola rubbed the back of her neck. "I, uh, don't know if I can really do this. I'm kind of scared that I'm in over my head."

Evelyn chuckled.

Viola frowned. "What's funny about that?"

"Not funny per se. I just remember the same 'in over my head' speech when you were in culinary school. You were so worried you couldn't keep up with the other students. And how did that turn out?"

Viola chewed her lip, and one corner of her mouth inched

upward. "I graduated at the top of my class."

"Exactly." Evelyn pushed a strand of Viola's hair away from her face. "There is no limit to what you can achieve if you can believe it. I have total faith in you. Maybe you should, too."

A sense of calm crept in, and Viola felt that her mother's support gave her strength and resolve.

The alarm on Viola's smartwatch beeped, and she straightened.

"I have to go." Viola stood and scanned the room for her purse. "I have a shift at the hot chocolate stand."

"Okay, dear." Evelyn swiveled her wheelchair and drove it toward the front door. "Don't forget your scarf. It's supposed to be cold later."

Viola threw on her coat and grabbed her scarf. "Thanks, Mom. Text me if you need anything. See you tonight."

Though they had messaged each other every week and spoken on the phone a dozen or so times in the last year, Holly missed spending time with her best friend, Kim. Kim's friendship was the only good thing Holly still had from her life in the big city.

Holly offered to pick up Kim from the airport, but Kim insisted that she "New York" it by taking an Uber. Kim had also turned down Holly's offer to let her stay at the cabin, claiming she didn't want to be in Holly's way. Holly felt it had more to do with having room service and the housekeeping staff at her disposal.

The plan was for Kim, Rachel, Avery, and Lucy to meet Holly in the town square so they could venture to the Blossom Boutique for their dress fittings. It had been a month and a half since Holly had most recently tried on her wedding gown, and she was filled with a mixture of exhilaration and anxiety at the prospect of doing it again.

Marie, the seamstress and boutique owner, had Kim's measurements to tailor her bridesmaid's dress, having measured Rachel, Lucy, and Avery in person. Today would be the first time the entire bridal party would have their dresses on simultaneously.

In the town square, Holly shivered as an icy breeze whipped at her hair. When her phone buzzed, she pulled it out of her coat pocket.

> Kim: I'm in the Uber now. I should be there in fifteen minutes.
>
> Holly: I wish you would have let me pick you up.
>
> Kim: Honey, no. You've got enough going on. I'll be there soon. No big deal.
>
> Holly: Hope your flight was okay.
>
> Kim: OMG!! Cutest flight attendant ever. Flirting with me big time.
>
> Holly: LOL Of course he was.
>
> Kim: See you soon.

Holly laughed as Kim ended the conversation with a kissy face emoji.

The next thing she knew, someone was covering her eyes with fuzzy gloves and saying, "Guess who."

Holly recognized the voice and smiled. "Hi, Mr. Mason."

Nick's father removed his hands and chuckled, his laugh sounding like a *ho-ho-ho*. He was notorious for being mistaken for Santa Claus, given his round belly and white beard. He even had a twinkle in his eye.

"Now, now. You call me Nicholas. Or Dad, if you prefer. Might as well get comfortable with it, future daughter-in-law."

"That's true. I think it might take some getting used to, though."

"Rachel told me to say she and Avery will be here soon."

"Message received." Holly patted his shoulder. "How are you doing?"

Nicholas Mason had been managing his Wilson's Disease with medication. Still, he tended to get fatigued easily and sometimes suffered from muscle stiffness. Thanks to the money from the tree decorating contest the year before, he could pay for his treatment for many years to come.

"I'm great," he replied. "I always get a little extra energy this time of year. I love the holiday season."

Holly grinned. "I can tell."

"Where's your mom? I still haven't met her."

"She's at the cabin. She's preparing something for later. Emily—um, Mrs. Weedleman and Mrs. Miranelli are there, too. They're all catching up."

"That's nice. I guess I'll meet her at the family dinner, then." He leaned closer. "You're still coming, right?"

Holly placed a hand on his arm. "Wouldn't miss it."

Mr. Mason shifted, and the grin faded from his face. At first, Holly wasn't sure what had changed and, for a moment, feared it was his health condition. But when Mr. Mason dug out his phone and squinted at the screen, she understood.

"I'm afraid I'm not very good at this texting thing." He snickered. "Can you hold this for a second while I search for my reading glasses? I thought I put them in my pocket, but—"

Holly took the phone. She couldn't help but look at the screen. "It's from Rachel. She and Avery need help at the shop."

Mr. Mason pulled his glasses from his inside coat pocket seconds too late. "Oh, all right. Thank you, dear."

Holly handed him back the phone. "My pleasure."

"I'll head to the shop, then. See you later, Holly."

She waved as he headed to The Gingerbread House.

"This town is the cutest." Kim's nasally voice floated to Holly.

Holly had to smile. Kim always sounded like she was whining, even when saying something positive. She turned to find her friend walking toward her, rolling her suitcase at her side. The faux fur hood of Kim's coat entangled with her dark, curly hair. Her eyes were bright as she took in the festival setup.

"Hi, Kim." Holly closed the distance between them and embraced her friend. "I missed you so much. Wait, did you get taller?"

Kim giggled as she stood back from the hug. "It's my shoes. Platform winter boots are my new favorite thing."

"Well, they look great on you."

Kim grabbed Holly's hands and stretched her arms out. "And you look fabulous. Whatever they've put in the water is really agreeing with you."

Holly laughed. "I think it's just the fresh air."

"Or maybe love," Kim teased. "Oh em gee! That hot chocolate stand, which is literally a standing cup of hot chocolate, is so utterly adorable."

"You want to get one? I kind of know the owner."

"Is it Nick?"

Holly waggled her brows. "Yep."

"Sweet lord. He really is a catch, isn't he?" Kim hooked her arm through Holly's. "Yes. Let's indulge."

Holly led her to the hot chocolate mug-shaped stand and waited behind the customer at the counter.

"How's the hotel?" Holly asked.

"So quaint."

"Uh oh. That's Kim-speak for small."

"No. It's fine." Kim raised a dismissive hand. "It's dripping in

Christmas decorations, and the staff is super nice."

"It's still two weeks until the wedding. Were you able to take off the whole time? Or do you have to go back in between?"

"I managed to take off between now and New Year's Day, and then I have to head back to New York. Since the promotion, I have been working my butt off, including some overtime on the weekends. And I was sure to remind them of that."

Holly playfully rolled her eyes. "Of course you did."

"So, you know, they couldn't say no."

Holly patted her on the back. "Well, I'm just glad you made it."

Kim giggled. "And who knows? Maybe I'll meet myself a gorgeous, rugged mountain man and never go back. Just like you."

Holly tiptoed in front of the window when it was their turn to order. "Hi, Viola. We'll have two double luscious hot chocolates, please."

"Sure," Viola said. "Coming right up. How are you doing?"

"Fine, thanks," Holly replied. "How are things going with you?"

Viola nodded. "They're coming along. No worries."

Holly smiled at her, relieved.

Viola turned around to prepare their drinks and reappeared moments later with the order. "Here you go."

Kim took her mug and sipped the chocolate drink.

Holly handed Viola some cash. "Viola, this is my friend Kim from New York. Kim, this is Viola. She's catering the wedding."

Kim took another sip. "Mmm. Cool. Hey, if you're serving these at the reception, I'm all for it."

Their attention was drawn to the sound of a crane in the middle of the town's square raising the peak end of a twenty-foot fir tree from a flatbed truck. Wearing a yellow construction helmet, Nick stood overlooking the task, his arms gesturing as he called out instructions.

Holly sidled up closer to Kim and pointed. "That's Nick."

Kim gasped dramatically and then whistled her approval. Always over the top, just like Holly remembered.

"He seems to know what he's doing," Kim said.

Holly laughed. "That he does." She gazed at him fondly as he removed the helmet and ruffled his hair. "He's a good guy."

Nick happened to look their way, and Holly waved. Nick returned the gesture with a coy smile. Holly stuck her thumb out at Kim, and Nick gave her a bow.

"Aw, he's so sweet," Kim said, her voice whiny again.

Holly felt her heart warm. "He really is."

"Oh." Kim nearly choked on her hot chocolate. "Speaking of good guys and bad guys, remember I texted you that I had something to tell you?"

"Honestly, I forgot about it, what with all the wedding planning going on."

"Yeah, well, I also didn't want to bother you with it. Especially if it amounts to nothing."

Holly braced herself. "Now you've got me intrigued. What's this about?"

"It wasn't me who leaked the news, but somehow Grayson got wind of your engagement."

Holly shrugged. "That's fine. I don't really care about Grayson or his opinions anymore."

"Which is totally mature of you and super smart. But the problem is he's really peeved with the whole thing and said—and I'm quoting him here—he'll be damned if you marry that 'small-town nobody.'"

"What?" Holly scoffed. "What a jerk. First of all, he doesn't even know Nick. And second, who does he think he is? What I do and whom I marry is none of his concern."

"I know. I just thought I should tell you."

"He said this to you?"

"Yeah." Kim arched a brow. "The moron had the nerve to come to my office demanding I tell him where you are. He must have heard about the engagement from mutual friends or something, and now he's hellbent on stopping the wedding. As if. He wouldn't stop going on about how you were going to regret leaving him. Delusional! But don't worry. I didn't tell him where you are."

"Thank you." Though she was relieved to know Kim had kept her location a secret, she couldn't help but grasp her stomach as it tightened with unease. *Could Grayson be a threat? But there's no way he could find me. Right?* She clutched her mug and told herself to stop worrying about someone who was miles away.

"So where is the other bridesmaid and your maid of honor?" Kim asked.

Holly was glad to change the subject. "Actually, Nick's sister would be *matron* of honor since she's married."

"Look at you, Ms. Wedding Facts Expert." She raised her hot chocolate. "Cheers to that."

Holly took a swig of her drink, hoping the warm liquid would help ease the churning in her belly. "They should be here soon. Rachel's at the eatery taking care of something, so I'm sure she'll be here soon. Knowing Lucy, we just have to keep an eye on the churro stand to see when she arrives."

"Lucy sounds like my kind of gal. And where's your mom?"

"She's at the cabin making *lumpia* for after the dress fitting."

Kim did a little hop. "Are those the eggrolls?"

Holly laughed at Kim's excitement. "Yes."

"Yum! I can't wait. I haven't seen your mom since—" Kim's smile faltered. "Well, since your dad's funeral."

Holly nodded. She controlled her breathing, not wanting to feel sad on a day that was supposed to be fun. Kim sensed her dismay and reached out to squeeze her hand.

"Holly!"

Holly turned at the sound of Avery's voice. The young girl hurried to greet Holly, her wavy brunette hair and the pompom of her winter hat bouncing as she ran. Avery's dimples deepened as she giggled. Not too far behind her came Mr. Mason, his grin emphasized by his rosy cheeks. He was accompanied by Dasher, Avery's dog and Cupid's sibling, who donned a red and white bandana around his neck.

"Avery, hi." Holly welcomed her with a hug. "This is my friend Kim."

Avery looked up at Kim with wide eyes. "The one from New York?"

"That's me." Kim nodded. "Nice to meet you, Avery."

Dasher was the next to reach them. He sniffed Holly's boots first before moving on to inspect Kim.

"You weren't kidding about the cute dogs." Kim crouched down and scratched Dasher near his ear.

"I see I'm late to the party." Mr. Mason let out his signature *ho-ho-ho* chuckle.

Kim stood upright and gasped. "No. Way. Did anyone ever tell you you're the spitting image of Santa Claus?"

"Once or twice." Mr. Mason winked and stuck out his hand. "Nicholas Mason. Nicky's father and Avery's grandfather."

"'Nicky'?" Kim slipped back into her whiny tone. "Oh my God, I love that."

"I like your purse," Avery said, running her fingers along the rhinestones bedazzled along the leather.

"Thank you." Kim beamed.

"I have a backpack with these stones on it. It's my favorite."

"Awesome. Sparkle power!" Kim raised her hand for a high five.

Avery hit her hand, and almost immediately, Dasher lifted his paw as if wanting to join in.

"Coolest dog *ever*," Kim exclaimed, crouching down to high-five.

Holly started when a figure rushed toward her. She knew it was foolish to think that Grayson would be there to pounce on her, but it was the first thought that popped into her head. She placed a hand on her chest and blew out a silent breath when she realized it was Lucy. Her blonde hair was neatly coiffed into a French braid, and her gentle gray eyes were filled with excitement.

"They have a new flavor of churro." Lucy said it as if it were the news of the century. "This is the happiest day of my life."

Kim turned to her with a smile.

"Kim, Lucy," Holly said. "Lucy, Kim."

Kim hugged Lucy. "Hi. So you're Holly's childhood friend whom she had a falling out with when she left to be a big-time artist."

Lucy let out a small laugh. "Yes, because she basically cut me out of her life for a while. But she returned and begged for my forgiveness, so now it's all water under the bridge."

"We gals are so dramatic, aren't we?" Kim joked.

Lucy shrugged. "Pretty much."

Kim settled a hand on Lucy's arm. "And you're excited about a new flavor of churro?"

"Absolutely, I am."

Kim rested her hands on her sides. "We're going to get along just fine. What's the new flavor?"

"Strawberry cheesecake."

"Oh my goodness." Kim held up a finger. "Holly, I'll be right back."

"I'll help," Lucy exclaimed.

"Grandpa?" Avery looked up at him with doe eyes.

Mr. Mason chuckled. "Say no more. Churros it is."

Just as they walked off, Rachel appeared, looking flushed. "Hey, Holly."

"Rachel, are you okay?"

"It's nothing." She shook her head. "I was just unloading a delivery before with my dad, and I think I overdid it with the carrying."

"Oh, no. I could have helped," Holly said. "Or I could have gotten Nick."

"No, no. I just need to catch my breath."

"Well, you didn't have to rush."

"Yes, I did," Rachel insisted. You don't know how much I need some girl time for a change. I'm so ready to try on our dresses and talk about wedding details."

"Well, I can make that happen." Holly pointed to the churro stand. "We're just waiting for the rest of the gang to get their much-needed snacks."

Rachel nodded. "Looks like they're hitting it off."

"It does."

When the rest of the gang returned, Mr. Mason gave them a nod. "You gals enjoy the dress fitting. I'll see you later."

"Bye, Mr. Mason," Holly called.

"Later, Grandpa." Avery waved.

"See ya, Santa," Kim added.

"Okay," Holly said to them. "Let's get you into some dresses."

Chapter Eight

Holly had fluttery sensations in her stomach. Her wedding gown only needed a slight alteration, and the seamstress promised she'd finish it in time for the wedding. Holly's bridal party lucked out, and they were able to leave the shop with their dresses. To top it off, Avery loved her flower girl dress so much that she had to be bribed into taking it off.

The chatter level in the car on the drive home rose parallel to the degree of excitement. Holly smiled to herself, glad that the members of her entourage were getting along so well.

She pulled into her driveway as the sun began to set. Holly's mom opened the front door as everyone made their way to the cabin, grinning broadly.

Kim waved at Vivian. "Hi, Mrs. St. Ives."

"Hey, Mom," Holly called out. "How was your day?"

"Good. Got my cooking done." Vivian waved cheerily. "Hello, girls."

"Whoa." Kim held her arms out at her sides as if steadying herself. "Something smells amazing."

"What is that?" Lucy approached the door wide-eyed. "My mouth is literally watering."

Vivian laughed. "Why don't you come in and find out?" She stepped aside to allow room for the guests to enter the house.

Kim hugged Vivian before stepping into the house. Vivian rubbed her hands together as the rest of the group shuffled through the door.

Holly giggled and hugged her mom. "You're so cute, Mom."

Vivian squeezed her. "How was the fitting?"

"I wish you could have come." Holly dug out her phone. "They have to tighten some of the beading that seems loose, so they're holding it a bit longer. But Kim took pictures."

Vivian *ooh*ed and *aah*ed at the shots of Holly in her gown. The smooth, ivory material fit her perfectly. The mermaid cut complemented her figure, and the intricate beading at the bodice gave the dress a regal touch. Holly swiped to the next picture, where she posed, looking over her shoulder, displaying the plunging back of the gown. A tingling spread through Holly's chest, radiating to the rest of her body.

"You look absolutely stunning." Vivian gave her one more hug. "Let's go inside. It's freezing out here, and the others are waiting."

When they strode into the house, they found Lucy and Kim standing by the table. Emily and Mrs. Miranelli sat on the couch with cups of steaming hot chocolate in their palms. Avery rested on the floor, flipping through an art book on the coffee table, and Rachel warmed herself by the fire.

After greeting the women who had spent the day with her mom, Holly approached the dining room table, and her eyes widened. Her mother had gone all out and made two huge serving platters of a Filipino stir-fried rice noodle-and-vegetable dish called *pancit*, and three platters of Filipino eggrolls called *lumpia*. The only things on the table Vivian hadn't made were the Christmas-themed cupcakes from The Gingerbread House, which Nick had baked himself.

Holly smiled but shook her head. "Mom, you weren't supposed to make a banquet."

"It's nothing. Go on, have some." Vivian tossed her head, her chin pointing the way to the feast. "Don't let it go to waste."

"Oh, it won't," Lucy said. "Believe me."

"Preach!" Kim added.

After Lucy and Kim filled their plates, the rest of the ladies came to the table to help themselves.

"Oh em gee," Kim said with a mouthful of food. "This is incredible."

Lucy nodded, her eyes wide and mouth too full to remark.

The others agreed as they indulged, and for a few minutes, no one spoke. All that could be heard was chewing and sounds of delight.

Mrs. Miranelli plopped down on the arm of the sofa. "How are the wedding preparations going?"

"Despite the hiccups," Holly began, "they are coming along. We just finalized the menu with Viola, and we got confirmation that all eight of Cupid's siblings will be attending."

"What?" Kim scoffed, nearly spitting pancit everywhere. "That's quite a number of dogs for a wedding."

Holly waved a hand. "Yes, I know. But Cupid is our ring bearer, and Nick thought it would be cute if all Cupid's brothers and sisters were there to watch his proud moment."

"That's adorable," Emily said. "Especially the part about Cupid carrying the rings to the altar."

Rachel shook her head. "Leave it to my brother to have ideas that are both adorable and corny at the same time."

"I have to say," Lucy chimed in, her mouth finally free of food, "we are going to be one heck of a gorgeous bridal party. I *love* our dresses."

"Heck yeah," Kim agreed. "Very flattering and chic."

Holly smiled to herself, glad that the attire aspect of the ordeal had worked out. The muted cornflower blue, chiffon gowns were in a Greek-goddess cut, the skirts elegantly flowing to the floor. She had been joyfully astonished when she'd seen her friends standing together in the shop, looking fabulous in the dresses she'd picked out.

When Holly looked over at her mother, she couldn't quite read her expression.

"What, Mom?" Holly asked.

Vivian tilted her head. "Maybe later."

"Maybe later what?" Holly laughed. "Come on. You're making me nervous. You don't like the dresses?"

"Oh, no, it's not that."

"What, then?"

"So, I know you already have a wedding gown, which is so gorgeous," Vivian began, "but I did bring you something you might want to, um, consider."

"Consider? What is it?"

Vivian got to her feet and raised her index finger. "Be right back."

Holly looked around, particularly at Emily and Mrs. Miranelli, who had spent most of the day with her mom. Perhaps she had shared the details of this surprise with one of them, though their expressions said otherwise.

Moments later, Vivian reappeared with a garment bag.

"Mom, what is that?" Holly stood and took two steps toward her mother.

Instead of answering, Vivian giggled. "Kim, can you help me?"

"On it." Kim stuffed the rest of the *lumpia* she was eating into her mouth before jaunting to Vivian's side.

"Hold this, dear." Vivian held out the garment bag to Kim so she could grasp the top. She then pulled down the zipper and took out what was inside.

Holly gaped as Vivian revealed an ivory, organza, and satin dress. The elegantly embroidered bolero-style top puffed out at the shoulders into loose satin sleeves. The high-waisted, floor-length skirt was smooth, almost shiny, and widened at the hem, with a tulle underskirt peeking out at the bottom.

"Is that a wedding dress?" Lucy asked.

"It's akin to traditional wedding attire." Vivian shifted so everyone could see the dress. "The traditional outfit is called a *Baro't Saya*, and it's actually not a dress at all, but a top and skirt."

Holly tapped her fingers on her parting lips. "Mom, it's beautiful. But I already—"

Vivian waved a dismissive hand. "I know. I know. It's just that sometimes brides like to change into another outfit for the party. You know, after all the formal pictures have been taken. And you would look amazing in this."

"Oh, you would," Rachel said.

The room was filled with murmurs of agreement. The women stared at Holly.

Holly ran her hand over the silky material. She didn't know if she'd be up for changing out of her chosen gown before the reception. It wasn't the easiest piece of clothing to get into, let alone get out of. But there would be no harm in having this dress on standby, just in case.

"Thank you, Mom. It's glorious. This must have been expensive."

"I only had to pay for the fabric." Vivian stuck out her chest. "Your Auntie Seng made it for you."

Rachel gasped. "Without her measurements? Or did she somehow have them?"

"That's how great she is." Vivian beamed with pride. "She based the dimensions on a picture of Holly and me standing beside each other. Also, Holly's got a cousin about the same size. And I said I could alter it if necessary."

Holly's eyes widened. "I'm speechless. I can't believe she made this. And I can't believe you brought it all the way over from the

Philippines."

"Honey, of course." Her mother placed a hand on Holly's cheek. "I'd do anything for you."

"I think it looks like a princess's dress," Avery said.

"I want to see it on you." Lucy clapped her hands.

"Yes, put it on," Kim added.

Rachel took the fabric between her fingers. "I've never seen a traditional Filipino wedding dress before. It's lovely."

Mrs. Miranelli scooted forward. "I'd say your Auntie Seng could make quite the killing if she went into the dress-making business, assuming she hasn't already."

Holly looked around the room. Emily smiled at her, her hands folded in her lap. Though Avery's eyes were on Holly, she continued to twirl as if she were still wearing the flower girl dress. Kim nodded in encouragement.

Her mother stood before her with raised brows, patiently waiting for Holly's response. There was no way Holly could disappoint her.

"All right." Holly faced the eager women. "I'll try it on."

"Great." Vivian beamed as she gathered the skirt in her arms. "I'll help."

Chapter Nine

Fluffy tufts of snow drifted around Viola as she headed inside the farmer's market warehouse. Every Sunday, the indoor marketplace was filled with booths and tables stocked with local farmers' produce, plants, and jarred goods. Viola hoped to find some spices and ingredients that weren't available at the supermarket. With the big event approaching, she had to test the recipes she intended to make for the wedding reception.

As she reached for a handheld basket, a set of fingers collided with hers.

"Sorr—" She was cut short by the shock of seeing Jonas in front of her.

Jonas pulled his hand back and straightened. He had not noticed Viola, focusing instead on his phone's screen. He shoved the device into his inner coat pocket and gestured for her to go ahead of him.

"After you," he said.

Viola offered the smallest of smiles. *I guess I better learn how to get along with him.* "Thanks," was all she said before heading toward the first booth.

As she completed a purchase of fresh-cut herbs, something furry brushed by her legs. She turned to see one of Silverwood's Malamutes sauntering by with its owner.

"I swear that dog is everywhere," came Jonas's voice from behind her.

Is he following me or something?

"That's probably not the same one," she pointed out.

Jonas stepped closer to her, but his focus was on the dog. "You mean there's more than one of those shaggy hounds in this small town?"

"You don't know about the Malamutes?"

"Is that some kind of urban legend?"

"They're actually quite famous." Viola strolled toward the next stand. "They saved the Christmas festival last year. It was in the papers."

"I must have missed that."

"Really? It was a pretty big deal. Especially because all nine are named after the reindeer."

"Nine of them?"

Viola laughed. "Yeah. Pulling a sleigh with Rudolph leading the way, just like the song."

Jonas's forehead crinkled for a moment. "That's, uh, wild."

"It was pretty cool. I can't believe you live in Silverwood and didn't see it on the news."

"Well, I wasn't in Silverwood last Christmas." He shrugged. "I was in Billings. Working."

"Billings?"

"The Lakeside Chateau is only one of my endeavors. I also own a business in Billings and split my time between here and there."

"Even for Christmas? Don't you take off for the holidays?"

He lifted his chin. "There are no holidays when you've got multiple businesses to run."

Viola frowned. "Well, that's sad."

Jonas stuck his fists in his coat pockets. "That's business."

Not knowing how to respond, Viola moved to another stand.

Jonas disappeared for a while, and Viola assumed he'd left. But when she got to the next booth to purchase some fresh vegetables, she heard a tongue click and glanced over to discover Jonas standing nearby with his hands on his sides. He searched here and there, obviously unable to find what he needed.

"What are you looking for?" Viola asked, unable to ignore him.

"Eggplant."

"That's what I like about this stand." She pointed. "They put the eggplant over there near the other berries."

He chuckled. "Other *berries?*"

She gave him a half-shrug. "Yeah."

"An eggplant isn't a berry."

"Yes, it is. I mean, scientifically. Culinary-wise, of course, they're not the same. But it is, in fact, a berry. So are bananas, tomatoes, cucumbers—"

"*Cucumbers?*"

She raised her brows. "You don't believe me."

He narrowed his eyes. "It just seems highly improbable. Inconceivable, actually."

"Are you willing to bet on it?" She smirked. "Look it up."

He watched her for a second.

"Whatever. Believe what you want." She shrugged and stepped over to the pears.

Out of the corner of her eye, she noticed Jonas taking out his phone. When he let out a muffled curse, she had to bite back a laugh.

She spotted some pears that looked amazing and moved over to that section, then froze when someone tapped her back, thinking it was Jonas and not knowing how to react. She whirled around and saw Oliver, then sighed in relief.

Oliver held up his hand. "Hey, Viola."

"Oliver. Hey, I meant to call you."

"Your mom needs me to do something?"

"Actually, *I* do." She shifted the basket to her other hand.

"No problem." He stretched out his shoulders as if ready to tackle whatever task she had for him. "What is it?"

She cringed. "You available New Year's Eve day?"

"Does this involve me dressing up like Baby New Year? Because I'll need to call my cousin to borrow his costume."

"No, no. Nothing like that. This is more like a freelance job for a few hours."

"I could use the money." He crossed his arms. "What've you got?"

"You know Nick Mason and Holly St. Ives?"

"Of course."

"I'm catering their wedding."

"That's awesome." Oliver fist-bumped her. "Congrats on the gig."

"Thanks. So. I've got some people to help me in the kitchen, but I'm short a few cater waiters. You know your way around a kitchen and have experience serving at Le Ruban Rouge, so I thought—"

"Yeah, sure. Sounds good." He nodded once. "Count me in."

"That would be amazing. You're the best. I'll text you the details."

"You need any more waiters?" he asked. "I could check with my coworkers at the restaurant."

"That would be perfect. Thank you."

"I'll be in touch." He waved as he went on his way.

The heavy load weighing down Viola lightened considerably. She had her menu ready and had already placed orders for supplies. Now that she was securing staff for the event, she believed everything was falling into place.

I could actually pull this off. Her pulse quickened, and there was a slight hop in her step as she palmed a couple of pears for her basket.

"This is unacceptable."

Viola turned at the sound of Jonas's voice. His back was to her, and he was facing the produce table. *Is he still making a big deal about the eggplants?*

"You're going to have to accept it," Viola said to his back. "It's a scientific fact: eggplants are berries."

When Jonas faced her, his forehead was scrunched into wrinkles. He glared at Viola and pointed to the Bluetooth device in his ear. "No, Steve. The overhead is too high. Tell them to draw up a new proposal and email it to me first thing tomorrow."

"Sorry," Viola mouthed.

Jonas pursed his lips and twisted away from her. "I don't care if they have to work all night." He stomped toward the checkout, one solitary eggplant in hand.

Viola tucked her hair back, checking to see if anyone had witnessed the exchange. "Okay, then. Never mind."

Chapter Ten

"Don't forget to clean up your station," Holly called out to the class. They'd been working with acrylics for the last forty-five minutes, and paint splashes littered the room.

The Silverwood Art School for Children students finished tidying up and left the room. Holly moved toward Avery, who was wiping down the base of her easel.

"I love your painting." Holly eyed Avery's canvas. "That combination of colors is so tranquil."

"Thanks." Avery chucked her wet wipe in the trash and untied her apron. "It came to me in a dream."

Holly's eyes widened. "Ooh, an art dream. It's so awesome when that happens."

Avery grabbed her backpack. "You have them too?"

"Yeah. Not all the time, but when inspiration wants your attention, it will find you somehow, right?"

Avery giggled. "I like that."

"Is your mom getting you today?" Holly asked as she walked with Avery out of the room.

"She's feeling a little sick. Something she ate, I think. Or a tummy bug."

"Oh, no. Well, I hope she feels better soon. So your dad's coming?"

"No, Grandpa's picking me up in his cool car."

"Lucky you. He still owes me a ride."

Avery smiled. "I'll remind him."

As they reached the hall, Holly grinned. As a former student of the school, Holly had been given the opportunity to take over from the owner—and her favorite teacher—Emily Weedleman, who had found Holly to be a great fit for the job. Apart from having a passion for everything artistic, Holly's stint in the art world had been successful, even if it was short-lived. She had since discovered a fondness for working with children, too, and taking over the school was the perfect chance to do what she loved while putting her talents to good use.

Holly and Avery entered the lobby, where Holly took in the sight of a curly-haired toddler playing with a rag doll on the carpet.

"Samantha!" Holly approached the little girl. It amazed her how much she resembled Lucy.

"Aw, she's so cute," Avery said, crouching to touch Samantha's curls. "I wish I could stay, but Grandpa's waiting for me."

"I'll see you later, Avery. We're coming over for Christmas Eve dinner."

"Oh, good. See you then." Avery waved as she headed out the front door.

"Hey, Holly."

Holly turned to face Sean, who'd been on the couch checking his phone. He pushed his glasses up his nose and ran a hand through his dirty blond hair before standing to hug her.

"So good to see you, Sean." She gestured at Samantha. "My goodness. She's getting big."

"And she's getting demanding, too," Sean joked.

"Is that right?" Holly crouched a little, facing Samantha. "Are you a little princess, Sammy?"

At the mention of her nickname, Samantha used the edge of the couch to pull herself to a standing position and extended her rag doll to Holly.

Holly took the doll. "What? You're standing?"

"Yeah," Sean answered. "We've gone mobile."

"She's walking too?"

"Well, she's taken a few steps. Lucy and I hope she'll walk freely by the time Lucy's parents drive up for Christmas."

Holly handed back the doll to Samantha. "If you're as determined as your mother, I'm willing to bet you can make that happen. Can't you, Sammy?"

"Hey, no pressuring my kid," Lucy called out as she arrived from her classroom. "If you want her to be a flower girl, you'll just have to postpone the wedding a few months."

Holly laughed. "Don't tempt me. Samantha would make an adorable flower girl, but Avery's got the job covered."

Lucy scooped Samantha into her arms. "Avery's the perfect flower girl. And we just bought the cutest dress for Sammy to wear on your special day."

"I can't wait to see it."

The front door opened, and Kim charged in, shaking snow off her head. She held a to-go coffee in one hand and tended to her stray hairs with the other.

"You can't tell me that's a coincidence," Kim said.

"What?" Holly asked.

"I saw Mr. Mason, a.k.a. Santa's doppelgänger, in the parking lot, and suddenly, it starts snowing. I don't buy it. That man is definitely Santa. Or, at the very least, Santa adjacent."

"Hi, Kim," Lucy said to her.

"Oh em gee, is this your little one?" Kim smiled and waved at Samantha.

"Yeah, this is Samantha. And this is my husband, Sean."

"Nice family, Lucy," Kim said as she shook Sean's hand. "Nice to meet you. Your wife and I have already bonded over food."

Sean chuckled. "Lucy did mention she met her match. Nice to meet you, too."

"Holly, hon, you ready to go?" Kim took a sip of her coffee. "Your mom's waiting for us to pick her up."

"I just have to get my stuff."

"Do you need me to lock up?" Lucy asked.

"No, Gretchen is here. She's sorting supplies and has the key." Holly crouched again and smoothed Samantha's hair. "Bye, Sammy. See you soon."

"Say bye-bye, Samantha," Sean prompted.

Samantha stared at Holly but didn't say anything.

Settling into the passenger seat of Holly's car, Kim fastened her seatbelt and took a sip of coffee. "Samantha is *so* cute. I need some cuteness in my life."

Holly pulled onto the main road. "What does that mean? You want a baby?"

Kim scoffed. "No. I don't know what to do with a baby." She wrinkled her nose. "No, I thought maybe a dog? Dasher and Cupid are pretty cute, too."

"Kim, don't forget you live in a small apartment on the fourth floor of a building in New York City."

"A small dog?"

"Small dogs need to pee, too. Who's going to walk it? You work full-time, plus overtime, and you live alone."

"Well, maybe I'll have to change that fact."

"What?" Holly's eyes widened. "Is there something you're not telling me?"

Kim laughed. "Holly, you'd be the first to know if I were dating someone. And I would have brought him to the wedding."

Satisfied that her best friend wasn't keeping secrets from her,

Holly concentrated on the road. There wasn't much traffic between the art school and her cabin, so when she realized the car behind her was taking every turn she was taking, a chill ran up her spine.

"What are you doing?"

It took Holly a second to grasp that Kim was speaking. "What?"

"You keep looking in the rearview mirror." Kim tapped the mirror as if Holly didn't know what she meant.

"I, uh, I think that car might be following us."

Kim wrinkled her brow and glanced over her shoulder.

Holly gasped. "No. Don't look."

"It's fine. They can't see me."

"You don't know that." Holly shifted her grip on the wheel. "Could you see the driver?"

"No. This is a small town, though. Don't you recognize the car?"

Holly stiffened her jaw. "No. You know what? Maybe I'm just imagining things."

The turn for her street was up ahead. Holly could feel her heartbeat accelerate as she flipped the indicator.

I'm imagining things. I'm not being followed. There's no way Grayson found me.

When Holly made the turn, and the car behind her continued to drive straight, she loosened her iron grip on the steering wheel and let out a relieved sigh. She felt like laughing at herself for being ridiculous.

Great. Kim has made me paranoid.

After pulling into her driveway, Holly saw her mom peeking out the front door. Holly waved, and Vivian came out in her thick coat, smiling as she approached them.

"Hey, Mrs. S.," Kim said once Vivian had gotten in the back. "You ready for this big tree lighting thing?"

"I can't wait." Vivian buckled in. "Jake and I used to have so much fun at the festival. When they finally light up that tree? So beautiful."

"Sounds awesome," Kim said in her nasal tone. "So, is there, like, an afterparty or something?"

Holly didn't answer. She was too preoccupied with the car driving behind them.

Is that the same car?

"You're doing it again," Kim whispered.

Vivian edged forward. "What is she doing again?"

Kim twisted in her seat. "She thinks someone is following us."

"Really? Like in an action movie?" Vivian twisted to look behind them.

"Mom, stop looking." Holly shook her head. "It's probably my imagination."

Kim leaned closer to her. "You don't think it could be *him*, do you?"

"*Him* who?" Vivian stuck her head between them. "Who's *him*?"

Holly shot Kim a warning look, but her friend apparently chose to ignore it.

"Grayson," Kim replied. "Her ex."

"Grayson?" Vivian placed a hand on the edge of Holly's seat back. "Why would he be here? And why follow you?"

Kim turned more to face Holly's mother. "He wants her back. He more or less warned me he was going to ruin her wedding."

"But he doesn't know where I am." Holly fought to keep her voice calm. She didn't want to yell, but the thought of Grayson being in Silverwood troubled her. "There's no way he'd know where to look. I haven't even mentioned Silverwood on social media. This is probably just paranoia triggered by you telling me what he said. I let it get to me, that's all."

"Are you sure?" Vivian asked. "It frightens me to think you might be in danger."

"I'm positive," Holly said, not just to convince her mom, but also herself. "He's all bark and no bite. Trust me."

"You're right," Kim agreed. "There's no way that dummy could find you."

Holly exhaled slowly. She didn't want to believe Grayson could be a threat. She hadn't mentioned him to Nick when Kim had told her about Grayson showing up at her office because she didn't want him to worry. Plus, Holly had always made a point of *not* bringing up the topic of her ex-boyfriend to Nick. Leaving her exes in her past was important to her, and she didn't want the thought of Grayson to dampen the joy of planning their special day.

Holly glanced in the rearview mirror once more. "See. That car veered off. They're not following us." She stretched her neck left and right, letting out a steady breath and telling herself it was all in her head.

As they approached the town square, Holly relaxed a bit more. The square was crowded, and it took her a moment to find a place to park.

Vivian unbuckled her seatbelt after Holly had parked. "Oh, I just remembered how fun this is."

They all climbed out of the car. With the sun setting behind the mountains, the lights of the Christmas festival seemed intense.

"What is that yummy smell?" Kim asked.

The three of them entered the square, where twinkling fairy lights decorated every stand and booth.

"That could be anything," Holly replied. "There are so many delicious things being sold here. Roasted nuts, popcorn, crepes, churros—"

"Stop." Kim laughed. "You're making me want to move here just for this festival. It's absolutely the cutest."

Delighted laughter and enthusiastic conversation tickled Holly's ears.

"I agree. Everything looks and smells so good," Vivian exclaimed. "And look, there's your father's sleigh."

In the center of the square, the glorious sleigh Holly's father had built stood atop a red carpet in front of the unlit Christmas tree. Fairy lights were attached to it but not yet switched on, and Holly bet they were connected to the switch that would light the tree.

The little stage set up near the tree was adorned with lustrous green garland and bright red ribbons. Festivalgoers filled the area, buying treats and warm drinks.

Holly and her group passed a stand selling herbs and spices. The aroma reminded her that she hadn't eaten since that morning.

The cheery holiday music that played over the loudspeakers stopped abruptly, and then two seconds later, a small brass band performed "We Wish You a Merry Christmas." Spotlights shone on the stage, and Silverwood's mayor, Margie McGuire, stepped up to the mic. She waved at the crowd. The fur of her winter coat hood fluttered in the wind, but the woman's auburn hair barely budged an inch.

The crowd applauded as the band's song ended.

"That's the mayor," Holly whispered to her mom and Kim.

"Well, good evening, citizens of Silverwood," the mayor said into the mic.

The applause grew and then subsided when Mayor McGuire raised her hands.

"Thank you. And welcome to this year's tree-lighting ceremony. I'm particularly fond of this time of year, and I'm sensing, from all those smiling faces out there, that you are too. Before we begin, I'd like to bring up on stage someone you might be familiar with. Mr. Nicholas Mason Senior."

Vivian moved closer to Holly. "Oh, did you know he would be

up there?"

"No." Holly wiggled her fingers at him. "I had no idea."

"Last year," Mayor McGuire continued as she put a hand on Mr. Mason's back, "your amazing and generous support was integral in helping Mr. Mason receive the medical help he needed. Not only did you all pull together to get our glorious tree ready in time to win the state-wide decorating contest, but your dedication to donating the grand prize to fund Mr. Mason's treatment showed the true spirit of Christmas."

The crowd *whooped* and hollered.

"And, of course, we can't forget the team that made it all happen and gained a moment of fame for our town: the Silverwood Alaskan Malamutes."

Nick, Rachel, and the owners of the other Malamutes climbed the stage individually with their dogs on leashes. Nick nodded to Holly. The nine Malamutes sniffed each other, tails and tongues wagging, and some playfully pawed the other.

The crowd went wild, and the band played a quick chorus of "Jingle Bells."

Holly hoped none of the dogs would begin to howl. If one started, the rest would join in, and no one would be able to hear anything else. Luckily, the Malamutes seemed to be on their best behavior.

"To continue in the spirit of giving, I am happy to bestow the honor of lighting the festival tree to our very own Nicholas Mason Senior."

Holly smiled, clapping for her future father-in-law.

"Thank you, Mayor McGuire." Mr. Mason gave her a half-bow. "And thank you, fellow citizens. I can't believe I've never done this in all my years in Silverwood."

He chuckled, and laughter bubbled through the crowd.

"It's a privilege to light this year's tree." Mr. Mason rubbed his palms together and reached for the box sitting on the podium. The box contained a big red button, which Mr. Mason pushed with bravado.

Vivian gasped as the lights on the tree came on. For a minute, everyone was silent, and Holly felt as if magic filled the air. The crowd applauded, and the band played another song.

The mayor and everyone on stage waved as they walked out of the spotlight and joined the masses. As amusement and conversations started up again, Holly glanced around. Her skin crawled as if someone were watching her, causing her to rub her arms and scan the crowd.

It's probably just someone I know spotting me from across the square.

But she didn't see anyone special looking her way. Holly shivered and moved closer to her mom, anxious for Nick to hurry through the throng of people to join them.

"Are you okay?" Vivian asked.

Holly didn't want to seem any more paranoid than she already was, and she didn't want her mom to worry when there was probably nothing to worry about.

"I'm just cold," Holly lied.

When she looked around again, she spotted Nick heading her way. As he wound his way through the crowd, saying an occasional *hello* to those he passed, Holly's muscles relaxed.

"Hey," Nick said as he reached her.

Cupid sniffed Holly's boots and sat beside Nick. Before she could utter a response to Nick's greeting, Holly wrapped her arms around him and squeezed. She had the urge to be still and let the relief set in.

Nick placed a kiss on her head. "You good?"

She buried her head in his shoulder. "I'm just glad you're here now."

Chapter Eleven

Viola squeezed her pen and bent over a notebook in the chateau kitchen. "That would be perfect, Christelle. I'll text you the details. Okay. Bye."

She set down the phone and clasped her hands to her chest with a smile. Now that she'd secured a complete team for the catering gig, she could breathe easier.

Viola glanced at her laptop monitor, checking over the final menu proposal once more before emailing it to Holly and Nick. It was close to what they had originally planned with their former caterer, with additional special touches that were all Viola's. She was confident they would approve.

Despite chalking up wins, she still suffered spells of self-doubt. Whenever those moments hit her, she mentally recited the adage her culinary schoolteacher loved: *All progress takes place outside the comfort zone.*

Checking the time, she frowned. The tree lighting ceremony would be over by now. Though she hadn't arranged definite plans, she had hoped to bring her mom to the festival. It always warmed her heart how her mom's eyes lit up at the illumination. Viola made a mental note to take her mom to see the tree one night.

She stood from the small desk in the corner of the kitchen. A pile of papers in the inbox caught her eye. She grabbed the three unopened envelopes from the top of the stack. Going straight home would be more appealing than dealing with invoices, but a voice in the back of her mind nagged her not to put it off.

When she ripped into the second envelope, she gasped. "Oh, no. This isn't for me."

The correspondence was addressed to Jonas Brickman. Viola was willing to bet Mr. Brickman was still in the building, probably holed up in his office, shutting himself off from humanity. She could wait until the next time she returned to the chateau, but that nagging voice was at it again.

After slipping the paper back into the envelope, she began her journey to find Jonas's office.

A light shone in a corridor off the main room that led to the winter garden. Viola wondered if Susan might be in there. If she was, Viola could ask her to pass on the piece of mail so she wouldn't have to confront Jonas.

Viola stepped into the winter garden and looked around. The inverted-lotus-shaped ceiling lamp still burned, but the room was vacant and peaceful in the silence of the evening. Romantic. Comprised of floor-to-ceiling windows and glass doors, this was where Holly and Nick would exchange their vows. It was lovely, especially in the daytime, with its breathtaking view of the mountains across the lake. Viola remembered how excited Holly had been when she had told her about the charming white chairs she'd picked out for the guests, the ivory runner that would stretch out between the entrance and the altar, and how the place would be filled with pale, pink roses, lilacs, and freesia. There would even be a wedding arch the happy couple would stand beneath.

Holly had also disclosed that wedding bells had been installed a few years ago. It was a nice touch and a true selling point for business.

Viola sighed, musing over how lucky Holly and Nick were to have found each other. To have found love. Viola wondered if she'd ever be so fortunate.

Running her fingers over the envelope, Viola turned and continued her search for Jonas's office. When she couldn't locate it on the main floor, she decided to try upstairs.

The curved staircase stretched before her, the carpeted steps muting her footfalls as she ascended. Wall sconces provided a soft illumination in the hall on the second level. She went left, searching an unfamiliar corridor, and discovered a dressing room, which she assumed was intended for brides to prepare for their ceremonies. There were other rooms, but none were Jonas's office. She changed direction and explored the other end of the hall, the carpet muffling her footsteps. Silence pushed in on her. The building seemed to be empty.

Then, a bit farther along, the quiet finally broke. Jonas's firm voice filled the hallway in spurts of short sentences.

He must be on a call.

Viola slowed her steps, wondering if she should wait or come back later. She was about to leave when Jonas's tone grew more serious.

"Of course, I want to go back to Lacey, but I need to handle things here first."

Lacey? Does Jonas have a girlfriend? Viola rolled her eyes at her thoughts. *What does it matter? It's not as if I like him or anything.*

She hugged the envelope addressed to him against her chest and backed away. Three steps into her retreat, her elbow connected with something. By the time she swiveled her head to see the vase toppling from its pedestal, it was too late. Viola winced as the decoration crashed onto the floor and shattered.

"Let me call you back," Jonas said in his office.

Viola whirled around as he emerged, cringing at the sight of him. "Sorry."

Jonas's brow furrowed as his focus went from Viola to the shards of scattered ceramic. "Did you need something?"

"No. I mean, yes." She held out the piece of mail. "This got delivered to me by mistake."

Jonas took the envelope. "Did you open this?"

"I did. But it was an accident. What I mean is I opened it before I realized it wasn't for me."

He rubbed his jaw and glanced back at his desk. "And just now, were you listening in on my conversation?"

She raised her hands. "I didn't intend to."

He pressed his mouth into a straight line and breathed audibly through his nostrils. "You know, I don't appreciate nosy associates. Are you aware I filed a lawsuit against the catering company that worked here before you?"

"Uh, yes." *What is he getting at?*

"Do you know why?"

"No." *Why is he talking to me like I'm five?*

"I caught one of them going through files in my office."

"Oh." Viola shook her head. "Jonas. Um, Mr. Brickman. I swear, that's not—I wasn't snooping. I'm not like that. I don't actually care about … What I mean is, I don't know why you're giving me the third degree. I was simply trying to give you your mail." She hadn't meant for the last sentence to sound so aggressive, but she was upset at his insinuations.

Jonas studied her as he bit the inside of his cheek. "All right, then."

Before she could respond, Jonas turned on his heel and marched away from her, closing the door behind him.

Viola pinched her lips together. Sharp aches exploded at her temples. She spun and stormed back toward the kitchen.

"You're welcome, I guess," she muttered.

It had already been a long, tiresome day, and now Jonas Brickman had just worsened it. All she wanted was to go home and forget he even existed.

Chapter Twelve

Viola shut off the car engine and heard her phone buzz. Before checking her notification, she removed her gloves and shoved them in her coat pockets.

> Sina: Hey, big sis. What's up?

> Viola: About to earn my halo. I'm at the Pine Valley soup kitchen preparing to serve some hungry souls.

> Sina: I' m pretty confident you've already earned your halo, but good on you.

> Viola: Thanks. I'm about to go in.

> Sina: Do a good job. You know how I feel about wasting food, so make sure to serve big portions.

Viola stuck her phone in her purse and headed to the volunteer entrance of the building. Flurries drifted around her, and Christmas music floated out from the establishment.

This was the remedy she required. After numerous run-ins with Jonas, she wanted to clear her mind and open her heart to the community. She'd woken up with the longing to recapture the holiday spirit. Jonas was a Grinch, and Viola needed to distance herself from that energy.

The back door to the kitchen was propped ajar with a small, wooden wedge. Viola pulled the door open and found a bustle of activity. A dozen people in aprons moved about the kitchen like clockwork. She scoped the area, trying to figure out who was in charge. Her gaze landed on a familiar face. Rachel scurried about the kitchen, placing jars on shelves and moving empty trays to the dishwashing station. Her hair was twisted into a messy bun atop her head.

"Rachel." Viola waited for a man carrying a metal container of cooked potatoes to pass before she approached.

"Hey, Viola." Rachel added more rolls to the tray on the counter in front of her. "I didn't know you were volunteering tonight."

"Yeah. You know, the season of giving."

"That's great."

Viola glanced around. "So, where am I needed? Do I have to check in with anyone?"

"Consider yourself checked in." Rachel gestured to the left with her chin. "A couple of volunteers who've been here a few hours are leaving soon. They're out front on the serving line."

"Okay, you got it."

"I'll go out with you and show you where." Rachel placed the last of the rolls on the tray. "Have you done this before?"

"Yes, I have. But I don't mind a refresher."

"You can store your stuff in the back room. Just pick any of the free lockers."

Viola unraveled her scarf from her neck. "Great. Be right back."

After quickly locking her coat and purse in a locker and washing her hands, Viola followed Rachel to the main area, where a long counter was laid out with trays of food. The dining hall was filled with people, half of whom were sitting at tables, digging into their hot meals. The other half stood in line.

"Ah, wonderful. Another set of helping hands." Mr. Mason, who held a pair of tongs, patted Viola on her back, greeting her with a huge smile.

"Happy to help. This inexplicable urge to come here tonight has been nagging me all day. I could blame it on the week I've had, but something tells me this may be the universe's doing. Or fate."

"Maybe the magic of Christmas." Rachel replaced the empty tray by Mr. Mason with a full one. "What happened this week that's got you worked up?"

"I've had a couple run-ins with the guy who owns the Lakeside Chateau." Viola sighed. "He literally yelled at me. I don't know. It's like he's got a vendetta against me, and every move I make is wrong."

Rachel gave Viola an apron and exchanged a look with her father. "Oh. Well, I'm sure he doesn't have a vendetta or anything."

"Maybe you should talk to him," Mr. Mason suggested. "Maybe it's all a big misunderstanding. Jonas has always been very kind to me the few times I've spoken to him."

"Everyone is kind to you." Viola's mouth went dry. "Wait. Jonas? You know him?"

"A bit." Mr. Mason leaned closer. "You want me to put him on my naughty list?"

Viola laughed as she secured her apron.

"Okay, you two, cut it out," Rachel said, interrupting. "Dad, why don't you scoot over and take over dishing out the carrots, and I'll give Viola bread duty."

"Sure, sure." Mr. Mason passed Viola the tongs.

"So, pretty straightforward," Rachel said to Viola. "One roll for each person unless they want more."

Viola nodded. "Got it."

Rachel was focused on something over Viola's shoulder. Her eyes widened for a moment. "I think I'm going to help out back. Someone needs to start tackling those dishes."

"All right. See you later."

Rachel disappeared, and Mr. Mason grinned before scooting over to the carrot station, tagging out one of the other volunteers.

Viola swiveled her head, wondering what had caught Rachel's attention. A pair of green eyes locked with hers.

Jonas Brickman. Of course.

At first, Viola didn't recognize him because he wasn't in a suit. Instead, he wore a burgundy sweatshirt, jeans, and tennis shoes. He appeared almost—dare she say it?—normal.

Almost normal. His flawless complexion spoke of an expensive skincare routine, and she was convinced his hair was under strict orders to remain in place at all times.

She grimaced, hoping he hadn't overheard her complaining about him.

Jonas acknowledged her with a nod before returning to his task of placing slices of roast beef on passing plates.

For a second, Viola's face, neck, and ears grew impossibly hot. She fidgeted as she averted her gaze.

Why, of all nights, does he have to be here tonight?

Viola adjusted her apron and pushed thoughts of Jonas away.

I'm here for the homeless, not to ponder Jonas Brickman's every move.

The line of patrons stretched along the counter and halfway to the front door. Viola forced herself to smile and exude a merry disposition as she used the tongs to pass out the rolls.

The faces of the grateful people receiving food filled her soul with a sense of purpose. She had to admit, she was also glad for the distraction from the intruding thoughts of Jonas. With each roll she placed on a tray, she felt a comforting calm take over.

After half an hour, Mr. Mason turned to her. "I'm leaving for the night. It's getting close to my bedtime." He chuckled.

"All right," Viola responded.

"You staying long?"

"I signed up until eight."

He settled a hand on her shoulder. "Don't stay out too late. See you at the shop."

"Yeah. See you. Have a good night."

A couple more volunteers came out from the kitchen to the serving line. There was a bit of commotion as people switched places, and Viola wasn't sure if she should stay where she was or move. One person came out and refilled her tray of rolls, and she took a step back to give them room. As she did, she bumped into someone.

"Sorry." Viola's face fell, and she felt the need to swallow the lump in her throat. "Um, Mr. Brickman. Hi."

"Hello, Ms. Carver." He situated himself at the station next to hers, ladle at the ready.

"What, uh, brings you here?" As soon as she'd asked, Viola's cheeks burned. *What a dumb question.*

Jonas Brickman smirked as he set down his ladle and retied the strings of his apron. "Same as you, I'm guessing."

"I would have never guessed you spend your free time helping the less fortunate. What a pleasant surprise."

"Are you kidding? I do this every year." Jonas grabbed his ladle and gave it a twirl. "You know, you really shouldn't judge someone until you get to know them better."

She opened her mouth to retort but quickly shut it again. He had a point. But it had been *her* point, and she was merely feeling sour that he had said it first.

After serving a few more patrons, she said, "It's just that you always seem preoccupied with work."

He gave her a sideways look. *Is he smirking at me?*

"Yes. I am. In fact, I'm going over the numbers of my year-end report as we speak." Jonas gestured at the dining hall. "But this is important, too."

He turned to smile at the people at his station as he scooped food onto their plates. Viola couldn't figure him out. Until now, she'd regarded him as a cold-blooded, money-driven robot with no soul. *Could Jonas actually have a heart?*

"How've you been, Sherry?" Jonas said to the woman in line.

"I'm surviving." Sherry's eyes were droopy, and her coat sleeves were torn.

"How's Carl?" Jonas went on. "Did he take care of that back of his?"

"You know Carl. Refuses to listen to anyone."

"You tell him to come see me." Jonas flashed her a smile. "I'll have a talk with him."

"You're kind, Mr. Brickman. I'll tell him. Don't you worry."

Viola placed a roll upon Sherry's tray and watched her move down the line. "Wow, who knew you were such a big hit among the masses?"

Jonas chewed the side of his mouth. "I'm willing to bet there's a lot you don't know about me."

"I suppose." Viola adjusted her grip on the tongs. "I mean, I guess the only thing I know about you is that you seem really stressed lately. Maybe even … grumpy?"

His eyes widened. "Oh. Okay. Grumpy."

"Yeah."

"Well, I've got a lot going on."

"Such as?"

"I mentioned I run a business in Billings."

She bit back a grin. "Hm, yeah. You did mention that."

"And I've got the chateau."

She waited. "Go on."

His brow furrowed. "Well, that's a lot."

"What about friends, family?" *Dare I say it?* "Committed relationship?"

He averted his eyes, rubbing his jaw before looking at her again. "I'm afraid my lifestyle doesn't leave much time for those benefits. To tell you the truth, splitting my time between here and Billings is literally me burning a candle at both ends."

"Well, maybe you should think about changing that." Viola couldn't believe she was being so bold.

"Now that you mention it, I'm considering giving up one of my endeavors. Selling one business so I can concentrate on the other."

"Okay, well, that makes sense. But you should also try to incorporate a little fun into your schedule. For instance, what are you doing this Christmas?"

"Working."

"What a surprise." Viola let out a huff of a laugh. "Do you even have a Christmas tree up in your house?"

He scoffed. "Do I *look* like I have the time to set up a tree?"

"You have time to do this." She gestured at the dining hall.

"This is a service. What will a tree do?"

"Lift your spirits?"

He raised a brow. "Highly unlikely."

She sighed and went back to her task. The conversation was going nowhere. *He's one of those guys who will never change.* She studied him again. He smiled at another patron, asking how their dog was. *Weird, though. He seems to be kind. There must be more there than what I'm seeing.*

At seven-thirty, Viola's legs were suffering the weight of her work. Someone came from the back and tagged her out. As she moved toward the kitchen, removing her apron, she was surprised to see Jonas following her.

"You're off, too?" she asked.

"I think four hours is sufficient. And they're shutting down in half an hour anyway." He held the kitchen door open for her.

"Thanks."

They went to the lockers, and Viola was tempted to get to know him better. It was like a puzzle she needed to unscramble. A code she had to crack.

"Hey, listen," she said to him as she wrapped her scarf around her neck. "I still feel bad about ruining your coat. The least I could do is offer you a coffee, on me. What do you say?"

He seemed to study her face, but she couldn't read him.

"That's considerate of you." He fastened his buttons. "But my coat's not ruined. See?" He ran his hand down the front of it. "All better."

"Still, I mean ... I know a coffee doesn't exactly amount to you having to get it drycleaned, but it's, you know, a gesture?" She wrung her gloves in her hands, and her toes curled up in her boots.

"It is a gesture. A nice one. As it happens, I've got plans." One corner of his mouth inched upward. "Raincheck?"

"Yeah. Yeah, sure." Her stomach twisted in a knot, and her cheeks were on fire. "Raincheck. Goodnight."

She couldn't leave the building fast enough. *What was I thinking? Inviting him out for coffee? And he probably has a girlfriend.* She swiftly got into her car and shut the door, burying her head in her arms over the steering wheel until her blush faded.

Chapter Thirteen

Holly awoke with a start. She hadn't had a nightmare in a long time. Wiping the sweat from her brow, she reflected on the dream.

Grayson.

Ever since Kim had told Holly about Grayson's outburst, she'd been uneasy. And last night, her brain had conjured up the image of Grayson chasing her through her old apartment building, screaming for her to stop. She'd woken from the nightmare just as he had been about to grab her.

She groaned as she stood from her bed. Shaking her head, she slipped on her slippers and staggered to the kitchen for some coffee.

Coffee's not going to be enough.

Once she checked the weather, Holly decided to go for a hike. A nice walk in the woods with Cupid should do the trick. Fresh mountain air always helped.

She dressed in layers and grabbed her backpack, complete with water and a first aid kit. Then, she whistled for Cupid. Nick's dog had been accustomed to spending the night at Holly's place from time to time, and she was glad he was there to accompany her.

After leaving a note for her mom informing her of where she would be, Holly left the cabin with Cupid at her side. The sunrise cast a faint glow over the trees, and the cool breeze smelled like pine and snow. Holly tightened her scarf and followed Cupid to the familiar path through the forest near her house.

Everything was quiet except for the crunching of her boots in the snow. As the sun climbed higher, the contrast between the dark green trees and the powdery white snow became stronger. Cupid picked up his pace and headed toward a small, babbling brook. Holly breathed in the fresh air, letting the peacefulness of the woods clear her mind.

She used to take these walks with her parents. For a moment, she wondered if she should have invited her mother to accompany her.

Up ahead, Cupid came to a halt, stretching his neck to sniff the air. He released a bark, which caused Holly to jump. A few thoughts ran through her head: a bird, a deer, a bear …

Grayson.

No. It couldn't be. That was paranoia and her latest nightmare taking over again. Still, she waited for a beat before she moved. Ears perked, Holly controlled her breaths. There was nothing to be afraid of. If it had been an animal, Cupid would have growled or chased it. He did have a penchant for running after squirrels.

Other than sniffing the air a bit more, Cupid didn't seem bothered. As he continued, panting as he traipsed, Holly sighed in relief.

Enough of the paranoia. You've got a bridal shower today.

She checked her watch. There was still plenty of time to enjoy her hike.

Three hours later, Holly and Cupid emerged from the woods. Her legs were achy, and the heels of her feet were sore. She anticipated stripping off her boots and soaking in a hot bubble bath. Cupid, on the other hand, seemed unfazed, trotting along happily as if he were just getting started.

When Cupid took off at a run, Holly barely had the energy to call after him. Luckily, she noticed Nick's truck parked in front of her place. He must have just arrived, and he seemed surprised to see her as he climbed out the driver's side.

"Hey." Holly waved as she came closer.

"Hi. Where have you been?" He kissed her on the forehead.

"I needed some air."

"I tried to call you. It's been three hours."

She grimaced. "I needed a *lot* of air."

He tilted his head. "Everything okay?"

She wrapped her arms around him. "Everything is perfect now."

On her tiptoes, she leaned in for a kiss. His lips were soft against hers, and a fluttering sensation spread in her stomach.

She didn't want the kiss to end, but there were still things to do before her bridal shower.

"What are you doing today?" she asked, continuing to hold on to him.

"Picking up my tux."

"Ooh, exciting."

"But first, I have to take care of some details for the Christmas festival."

"Sounds good. I need to get ready for the bridal shower. But first, I think a soothing bath is necessary."

He lifted one brow. "Well, I know where I'd rather be, but I've got to uphold my reputation as a responsible coordinator."

Holly released a breathy laugh. "Such a good boy."

"Yeah, well, I've kind of let my to-do list fall to the wayside since we've been dealing with all these wedding plans."

"Do I sense a bit of regret?" she teased.

He tugged her nearer. "Not a chance." He kissed her once more, deeply, before pulling away. "See you later?"

"You can count on it."

"Enjoy your bath. And your shower."

Chapter Fourteen

By the time the bridal shower was underway, Holly felt much more relaxed. It helped to be surrounded by friends and family in the comfort of her cabin. Along with her mother, Mrs. Miranelli, Emily, Lucy, Kim, and Rachel, some of her other close acquaintances and colleagues in Silverwood were in attendance. As Holly opened gifts, her spirits were lifted even more.

"This one is from Kim." Vivian placed the pink-and-white wrapped box in Holly's lap.

Holly sat in an armchair encircled by shiny, torn-up wrapping paper. She grinned as she ripped at the edges of Kim's gift. Under the fancy paper was an even fancier box. Once she got past all the perfumed tissue, Holly withdrew a black silk robe.

Kim smiled with her tongue between her teeth. "Thought you could use some New York vibes on your honeymoon."

"It's lovely, Kim. Thanks."

Vivian handed her the next gift.

"Who is this from?" Holly asked.

"It's from Nick."

"Nick? He wasn't supposed to get me anything." Holly ran her hand over the little box before she opened it. The box contained a velvet jewelry case, which she flipped open to reveal a silver chain-link bracelet with a snowflake pendant. It matched the necklace he had given her for Christmas the year before.

"He's so sweet," she remarked.

"There's a note." Emily gestured at the card.

Holly opened the card and read it aloud. "Holly, my love, to quote Virginia Woolf, 'In case you ever foolishly forget, I'm never not thinking of you.'"

Vivian squeezed a fist on her heart. Lucy and Kim gushed.

"I've got to hand it to my cornball brother," Rachel said. "He does have a way of saying the perfect thing at the perfect time."

Holly cradled the card on her chest. Her heart tingled, and she could swear she was floating.

"This is the last one." Vivian passed Holly the final gift from the coffee table.

"That's from me," Lucy announced.

"What could it be?" Holly took in the size and weight of the package. She couldn't assess what her unpredictable friend might have gotten her. After the wrapping paper had been torn away, she let out a laugh. "A food processor."

"That's right." Lucy pointed at it. "I expect you to put it to good use. I'll be over once a week to make sure of it."

Kim laughed and high-fived Lucy. "Nicely done."

"Well, I love it. Thank you." Holly looked around at all her guests. "I love all my gifts. You guys are the best."

"And this is just the bridal shower," Rachel put in. "I can't wait to see what you get for the actual wedding."

"I can't even imagine." Holly pressed her fingers to her temples. "I didn't even think about that. I've been concentrating on all the preparations for the ceremony and the reception. I totally spaced on the gifts and everything that comes after. Oh, my goodness, I'll have to pack for my honeymoon."

Mrs. Miranelli chuckled. "Well, that's the best part. Where are you kids going?"

"Jamaica."

"Oh, nice," Emily remarked.

Lucy whistled. "That's quite a drastic change of weather."

Vivian set a hand on Holly's shoulder. "Reminds me of my shocking honeymoon weather change."

"Where was that?" Rachel asked.

Vivian raised her hands, gesturing at the cabin. "Right here, in Silverwood. Jake and I were married in the Philippines. So, we did the opposite. Hot to cold."

"Sounds brutal," Kim whined, faking a shiver.

"Don't worry." Vivian winked. "We kept warm."

"*Mom!*" Holly covered her cheeks as the others giggled.

The chirp of Rachel's ringtone interrupted the laughter floating in the room. She held the phone to her ear. "Hey, Nick. What's wrong?" With wide eyes, she locked gazes with Holly.

Struck by Rachel's expression, Holly stood and crossed her arms. Everyone in the room went quiet, waiting.

"Oh, no." Rachel paced the small, crowded living room. "Where? I'm on my way."

Holly's heart thrummed in her chest.

"I have to go," Rachel said. She dropped the phone into her purse.

Holly shook her head. "What is it? What happened?"

"It's my dad." Rachel swallowed hard. "He's been rushed to the hospital. Nick's on his way there. I'm sorry. I have to go."

"I'll go with you," Holly insisted. "Mom, can you take care of things here?"

Vivian placed a hand on her arm. "Yes, of course. Go on." She nodded to Rachel. "I hope he'll be okay."

"Thank you," Rachel said.

Holly grabbed her keys and her coat. "Okay, let's go. I'll drive."

Chapter Fifteen

Holly spotted Nick as soon as she and Rachel entered the waiting room of the hospital's emergency center. His hair was disheveled as he ran his hand through it. When Nick noticed them, his jaw quivered.

Rachel rushed forward and hugged her brother. "What happened? What's going on?"

"He was having trouble breathing." Nick was pale. "We were at the shop, and he grabbed on to a chair to keep from falling. Couldn't get his breath back."

Holly covered her cheeks with her palms. "Oh, no."

"So I called 911, and they gave him oxygen, then brought him here. The doctors are looking at him now."

"Okay." Rachel swallowed, nodding. "It's going to be okay. He's in capable hands."

Nick bit his bottom lip, his head lowered. Holly touched his arm, and he pulled her closer for an embrace.

"Did you tell Eddie?" Nick asked his sister.

Rachel crossed her arms as she paced. "Yeah. He's at home with Avery. I told him I'd keep him up to date."

"I guess now we just wait." Nick gestured at the chairs.

The three of them sat, not speaking. Holly interlaced her fingers, fighting off the feeling of her throat closing up. The weight in her chest was almost unbearable.

She could imagine what was going through Nick's and Rachel's heads. They had lost their mother at an early age, and now their father was in the emergency room. The thought of losing him had to be soul-crushing. As the child of a widow herself, having one parent left to cling to was a delicate thing. One day, she would grieve her mother, and it would hurt just as much as when she lost her father. Still, she dreaded the prospect of something happening to her anytime soon, and she was positive Nick and Rachel felt the same about Mr. Mason.

Holly's phone buzzed. It was as if Vivian had known she'd been thinking of her.

"My mom's checking in. She says she prays everything is going to be all right. She sends her love."

Silence took over again. It seemed like they'd been there for ages when a doctor finally approached them in the waiting room. A surgical mask hung off her chin, and she had four pens sticking out of the pocket of her lab coat.

"Mr. Mason."

Nick stood. "Dr. Kim, how is he?"

"We gave him a steroid to help his breathing. There was no sign of distress to the heart. Everything appears to be all right, but we'd like to keep him overnight for observation because of his condition. There doesn't appear to be any jaundice, but it would be helpful to get a scan of his kidneys and liver just to be certain. We can check his blood count in the morning to ensure everything is as it should be."

"Can we see him?" Rachel asked.

"Yes, of course. We've set him up in a room. I can take you there." Dr. Kim gestured toward the hall.

Holly interlocked her fingers with Nick's. Her head was riddled with memories of when her own father had been hospitalized.

This isn't the same. Mr. Mason will be fine.

She frowned, trying to get her mind to stop racing through the possibilities.

When they reached the room, they found Mr. Mason lying in a hospital bed with nasal cannula tubes in his nostrils.

Mr. Mason smiled sheepishly and wouldn't look anyone in the eye.

"Hey, what's all this fuss?" Mr. Mason asked.

"Dad." Rachel came forward and hugged him. "Are you all right?"

"Just had some trouble breathing. They want to keep me for observation, but Dr. Kim thinks I'll be fine and can check out tomorrow."

"I'm so glad you're okay," Rachel said.

"You had us worried," Holly said.

"No need to worry about me." Mr. Mason winked. "I'm as tough as they come."

Nick sat in the nearby chair and took his father's hand. "That's not something you have to prove, okay? You need to take it easy."

Mr. Mason hesitated, his smile slowly disappearing. With a curt nod, he said, "Yeah. All right."

"They're keeping you overnight." Rachel pulled out her phone. "I'll let Eddie know I'm camping out here."

"No." Mr. Mason shifted in his bed. "You'll do no such thing. It's bad enough I'm in here. I don't want Avery anxious about when her mother will be home."

"I can stay," Nick insisted. He gave Holly a nervous look. "Cupid can sleep at Holly's tonight."

"Absolutely, of course," Holly said. "I'll pick him up on my way home."

Mr. Mason sighed. "You know I don't like all the bother. Makes me feel old."

Nick squeezed his father's shoulder. "It should make you feel loved. It's no bother for us, Dad, honest. Let us do this for you. You've taken care of us your whole life. Allow us to return the favor."

Mr. Mason nodded, his eyes welling with tears.

Chapter Sixteen

Viola's shoulders were strained from the heavy bags she carried into the chateau. Aside from the fresh produce that would arrive two days before the wedding, these bags contained the last of the non-perishable supplies she required for the reception preparations.

While Viola was stoked about all her plans panning out, she couldn't shake off her anxiety. She was counting on the logical part of her brain to take over, to concentrate on the job she needed to get done and to push past the part of her brain that was making her stomach churn and the muscles in her neck ache.

I can do this. All this hard work is going to pay off.

If this catering job proved successful, she could really make a name for herself. Her culinary dreams were within reach. She just had to press on a little longer.

As she walked through the building, a sweet, delightful scent drifted past her. Viola followed the smell to the kitchen, wondering what delicious smell emanated from the space she'd claimed in the chateau. Once she entered through the doors, she halted, surprised at what she saw. The last person she'd expected to find was Jonas standing at the counter, cutting into a pie tin.

He glanced at her over his shoulder as the kitchen's double doors swung shut. "Oh, hi."

Viola snapped out of her astonishment and placed one of the bags on the counter before she tucked a lock of hair behind her ear.

She blinked quickly as if that would help her process what she was seeing. The sleeves of his pristine white button-up shirt were rolled up to his elbows. His expensive suit jacket draped over the back of a chair, and he wore Viola's pink apron over his front. There was a smear of flour on his cheek, and apple peels littered the workspace.

"Hi." Viola furrowed her brow. "What are you doing here?"

He smirked. "It *is* my building."

"No, I mean here in the kitchen." She held up a hand. "Yes, I know. It's your kitchen. What's this?"

Jonas set down the knife and wiped his hands on the apron. "I made pie."

Viola put the other shopping tote on a stepstool by the refrigerator. "I didn't know that was something you did."

"I'm willing to bet there's a lot about me you don't know. My fondness for making pies is just one."

"*Fondness?*" She couldn't bite back her smile. "Okay."

"It's something I do from time to time, especially when I'm feeling bogged down from work. It's sort of like a meditation process, rolling out the dough and decorating the crust. Helps me relax."

"*Relax?*" She crossed her arms. "I didn't know you were capable of such a thing."

The smallest of smiles appeared on his face. "It's been known to happen on occasion."

"And pie-making fixes that?"

"I can permit my mind to be at peace for a while, deter me from becoming a total jerk who blows up at people."

Viola regarded him.

"I know you probably don't believe me, but I don't enjoy that tyrannical side that slips out when I'm stressed." He pursed his lips. "I'm sorry for being so rude to you."

She lifted a brow. "Which time?"

He let out a small laugh. "I deserve that, I suppose. How about this: I apologize for any time I've raised my voice or said anything disrespectful to you. I don't want to be *that* guy."

Viola uncrossed her arms, gazing into Jonas's eyes. He seemed sincere.

"Thank you," she finally said.

He nodded.

Viola gestured at the pie. "Well, it smells delicious."

"You should taste it to verify your suspicions." He picked up a fork, shoveled a hunk of pie, and held it between them.

"Taste it? You, uh, don't have plans for it?"

"I planned to eat it, but I'd rather not do it alone. Come on. It's cooled down enough. And I promise it's not poisoned."

"Well, the thought hadn't crossed my mind. But now that you mention it ..." She smirked before leaning forward.

At the last second, he retracted the fork. "Wait."

"What's wrong?"

He studied her face. "Close your eyes."

She felt a flutter in her stomach. "Why?"

"It intensifies the experience when you focus on fewer senses."

Why was her heartbeat accelerating? His gaze was enough to stop her heart.

He took a step closer, holding the fork near her mouth. In a soft whisper, he repeated, "Trust me. Close your eyes."

Viola's body quivered. She was very aware of her own breathing as she gazed back at Jonas. His eyes seemed to darken as he stared at her mouth. Their proximity sent a flutter to her stomach. She took a deep breath before lowering her lids and parting her lips. The scents of apple and cinnamon wafted up to tickle her nose.

It couldn't be more than a second, but somehow, the wait seemed infinite. As the warm pastry briefly brushed against her upper lip, she had to stop herself from letting out a moan.

Jonas slipped the fork into her mouth, and she wrapped her lips around it, taking in the explosion of flavors erupting all over her tongue.

Brown sugar? Cardamom? Is that butterscotch?

Viola opened her eyes as she finished the bite and was met with piercing, green eyes. So many emotions ran through her: euphoria from the best pie she'd ever tasted, surprise that Jonas could bake something so delectable, and a sense of trepidation from the intense way he gazed at her.

"I'm no culinary school prodigy, but I'm inclined to say it's pretty good." He shrugged. "What do you think?"

She swallowed hard, hoping her voice wouldn't fail her. "It's delicious. I'm impressed."

He didn't smile in response. Instead, his focus went to her lips. When he shifted closer, she didn't back away.

A buzz sounded. Viola blinked, and in the next second, Jonas reached into his back pocket and took out his phone.

Viola cleared her throat. "Something important?"

"Yeah." He returned his phone. "Susan texted to remind me of a conference call I've got in half an hour."

"Business calls." She gestured at the pie. "Won't that undo all the good the meditative baking was for?"

"Hopefully not. Besides, maybe this was all part of my master plan to invent the next best culinary creation."

"Actually, one of the most famous culinary inventions of our time was an accident."

He narrowed his eyes. "What was that?"

"The chocolate chip cookie. Its creation was an accident."

"Really?"

"Yep. Ruth Graves Wakefield, who owned the Toll House Inn,

wanted to make chocolate cookies, so she chopped up a chocolate bar into the cookie dough, expecting the chocolate to melt. Of course, when it didn't, she said she'd done it on purpose."

A grin tugged at the corner of his mouth. "It's crazy that you know that."

"Not really." She shrugged. "I learned it in culinary school."

"So this Ruth Graves …"

"Wakefield."

"Right." His brow arched. "She must have gotten considerably rich for inventing the most famous cookie on the planet. Even if it had been an accident."

"Well, she gave Nestlé the recipe and was paid with a lifetime supply of chocolate. But, you know, *rich* means different things to different people."

Viola grabbed the fork and took another bite of the pie. She turned to face him again when she felt his eyes on her.

"Yes, it does, I suppose," he replied.

She bit her cheek. "You think I'm weird for bringing up random food facts, don't you?"

"Actually, I find it endearing."

Her cheeks grew hot, so she attempted to shift the focus. "You know that's my apron?"

"I figured. I hope you don't mind me borrowing it. These pants are from Italy."

"I don't mind. It looks quite good on you." *Did I really just say that? Does he think I'm flirting with him? Wait. Am I flirting with him?*

Jonas ran a hand down the apron. "I always thought pink suited me."

"Definitely."

Viola's gaze fixed on his charming smile. She'd jumped to conclusions, thinking he was just some rich, arrogant bully. He was kind of sweet. And he made a damn good pie.

Everyone deserves second chances, right? I'd like to see more of the real Jonas. But I can't just ask him out. He might have a girlfriend. How can I suggest spending time with him—platonically?

It had to be something that he would consider a service, as he pointed out regarding the soup kitchen, otherwise he would turn it down.

She could feel her thoughts scrambling, making her somewhat dizzy. "So, listen," she started, leaning back against the counter. "I know you're all for helping out mankind—as demonstrated by your volunteering at the shelter—and I was wondering if you'd like to accompany me on another quest. In the spirit of Christmas, of course."

Quest is good, right? It's not a date.

"What kind of quest?" Jonas took a bite of pie and waited for her to explain.

"Silverwood Sky is selling day tickets and giving their proceeds to a kids' charity. I thought, if you have time, we could take part."

Her pulse thumped so hard she thought it would knock the kitchen walls down.

"Silverwood Sky? As in the ski resort?"

"Yeah. We could do a little skiing, take in a hot chocolate, maybe make a day of it. For charity, of course."

Jonas set down his fork. "I'm not really a big skier."

Her heart pounded in her ears as she was sure he would reject her proposition.

"Make a day of it, huh?" His eyes roamed over her face. "All right. I'm in."

Chapter Seventeen

Nick and Holly stood on Rachel and Eddie's front porch. Nick rang the doorbell, and Holly smiled as the bells chimed to the tune of "Angels We Have Heard on High." Cupid sat on his haunches, waiting for someone to answer. His breath caused vapors to float out onto the cool night air.

"Are you sure your father is up for this?" Holly removed her wool hat. "Shouldn't he be resting or something?"

"He insisted because it's Christmas Eve. You know how he is. Besides, the doctors said he was fine. They gave him the green light."

"All right. Good." Holly fidgeted with her scarf.

"Holly!" Avery immediately wrapped her arms around Holly's waist after opening the door.

"Merry Christmas, Avery."

"Merry Christmas. I'm so glad you're here." She widened her eyes dramatically. "I'm starving."

Holly laughed. "Okay. I can't decide if I should be flattered or not, but it's good to see you too."

Dasher ran to the door and barked. Cupid barked back and chased his canine brother into the belly of the house.

"Hi, Uncle Nick." Avery smiled up at him.

"Hey, kiddo. Merry Christmas." Nick ruffled her hair.

When Avery skipped off, Nick leaned closer to Holly.

"Am I not cool enough to get hugs anymore?" he whispered as they entered the house.

Holly rubbed his back. "Don't worry. You'll get extra ones from me."

A playful glint danced in Nick's eyes, his lips curling into a knowing grin.

A familiar chuckle from the living room entrance made Holly turn.

"Well, I see we've bumped up this party to a ten." Mr. Mason came forward and embraced Holly before placing a small peck on her cheek. "Merry Christmas."

"Ignored again," Nick joked.

Mr. Mason emitted a *ho-ho-ho* laugh and embraced his son, slapping him on the back for good measure.

"Merry Christmas, Mr. Mason." Holly placed a hand on his arm. "How are you feeling?"

"I'm right as rain, dear." Mr. Mason took her coat. "Don't you fret about me."

A figure moved into the foyer, redirecting their attention. It turned out to be Rachel's husband, Eddie, who nodded at them. His sandy-blond hair sat in waves atop his head. His knit sweater fit snuggly around his biceps as he stuffed his hands in his jeans pockets.

"Nick, Holly," Eddie called. "So happy you could make it. And, Nick, I could really use your magic touch with some of the dinner preparations."

"I'm beginning to think that's the only reason I'm invited over anymore," Nick teased. He pushed up his sleeves. "But if that's the price I've got to pay, get ready for some magic."

"Where's your mother?" Mr. Mason looked over Holly's shoulder.

"She's out with Rachel," Holly replied.

"Rachel? I was wondering where she was. What are those two up to?"

"They won't tell me. Probably some last-minute Christmas shopping." Holly shrugged and giggled. "But it's fine. I'm resolved to let the surprises come as they may."

Mr. Mason elbowed her. "More time for us to bond. Speaking of which, I could use your assistance."

Holly glanced over at Nick, who was elbows-deep in meal prep with Eddie.

"Absolutely." Holly hooked her arm through Mr. Mason's. "Lead the way."

He escorted her to a room on the ground floor she'd never been in. Judging by the bed, dresser, and desk, she deduced it was his bedroom. It was quite tidy, and Holly wondered if Rachel kept after him or if Mr. Mason was secretly a neat freak. Holly spotted bottles of his medication on his nightstand.

"What's up?" Holly asked.

"It's a little embarrassing," Mr. Mason began, closing the door, "but I can't get my fingers to work as they used to. I've been trying to wrap these presents, but my arthritis is getting in the way."

"No problem. I'd be happy to help." Holly sat at the small desk and rolled out some of the wrapping paper lying on the surface. "Now that we're alone, can you tell me how you're really doing?"

"I told you. I'm fine." He gestured to the first gift. "This one's for Avery."

Holly glanced up at him as she wrapped the paper around a jewelry box. She could tell he was attempting to change the subject. "She'll love it."

Mr. Mason fiddled with one of his shirt buttons.

"You know," Holly began as she finished taping the paper, "my father was also a stubborn man."

"Is that right?" Mr. Mason cleared his throat and handed her another box. "This is for Nicky. Don't tell."

"Yeah, he was." Holly refused to allow him to take the conversation on a detour. "And when he got sick, he hid it from us."

"Holly, dear. Really. I'm fine. I think I just got a little winded, caught up in the excitement of Christmas."

"I was really worried about you." She stood and squeezed his shoulder. "You're family to me. You're important."

Mr. Mason rested a hand on top of Holly's. His gaze was soft as he nodded. "You're important to me, too. I promise I won't hide it from you if I'm not feeling well enough."

"Okay, you better not." Holly pulled him in for a hug.

There was a knock at the door, and one second later, Nick appeared in the doorway with a suspicious face. "I hate to interrupt whatever mischief you two troublemakers are up to, but Holly, your mom's here."

Mr. Mason clapped his hands once and smiled. "Goody. Now the party can begin."

"I'll help you with the rest after dinner," Holly whispered to Mr. Mason.

"You're a star, Holly. Thank you."

Nick stepped aside and let his father out of the room, hanging back until Holly approached him.

"What was that about?" Nick tugged Holly closer.

"Oh, you know. The usual Christmas hijinks."

Nick shook his head. "Maybe I don't want to know."

Holly patted his bicep. "You're a wise man." She made her way to the kitchen, where she could hear her mother talking to Mr. Mason.

"It's so nice you caught up with Emily," Mr. Mason said. "Did you know that she and I went to school together?"

"What a small world." Vivian turned to see Holly approaching. "Hi, honey."

Holly stopped between her mother and Mr. Mason. "How was your outing with Rachel?"

"Lovely," Vivian answered.

"I had lots of fun," Rachel added. "Your mom is the best shopping buddy. I don't know if I've ever laughed so hard in my life."

"She finds my observations funny—" Vivian explained. "I'm just calling them as I see them."

Rachel simply pointed to her. "She's a hoot. I'm telling you."

"Where is Kim?" Vivian asked.

"Lucy invited her over," Holly explained. "I think they might be planning something. I figured I'd stay out of the way of their bonding and let them have their fun."

"You know when I first met Kim back in New York, I think she was afraid of me." Vivian raised her brows and nodded.

"What?" Holly giggled. "No, she wasn't."

"I guess *intimidated* is the right word, then." Vivian waved a dismissive hand. "She was pretty quiet and kept looking at me like I was going to yell at her."

"Maybe she just didn't want you to think she was corrupting your daughter," Holly said.

"Or," Nick began, "maybe she knew you were the only person who could convince Holly to leave the city, and Kim didn't want to lose her."

Vivian's eyes went from Holly to Nick. "Well, I'm delighted it was you who led her from the city, and for good reason. She's much happier now."

"All right, chatterboxes." Eddie approached, holding a roasted turkey on a platter. "Dinner's ready. Everyone, grab a seat."

"It smells delicious," Holly said. "Can I help?"

"Sure. You can bring the mashed potatoes over." Eddie gestured to a serving bowl on the counter.

Nick emerged from the far end of the kitchen with a casserole dish full of stuffing, which he placed on a hot plate in the center of the table. Rachel opened a bottle of red wine.

Avery hovered nearby. "Mom, can I sit next to Vivi?"

"Only if you behave." Rachel shot her daughter a playful warning look.

"Okay." Avery's giggle implied the opposite.

"It might not be Avery who has to be told to behave," Holly said as she took a seat. "I suspect my mom's been slipping her a piece of candy or two before dinner."

Vivian and Avery exchanged a secretive look as they sat beside each other. The rest of the group found their places and began filling their plates.

"Your house is beautiful," Vivian said to Rachel and Eddie. Her quick change of subject hadn't gone unnoticed. "So big. I bet I could fit all my brothers and sisters in it."

"Oh?" Rachel passed the bowl of mashed potatoes to Nick. "How many brothers and sisters do you have, Vivian?"

"I'm the second of ten." Vivian beamed.

Rachel's eyes widened. "Ten? That's incredible. Your mother must be quite a woman."

"Having that number of kids is pretty unheard of nowadays." Mr. Mason chuckled. "I do remember a time when big families were the norm. I'm the youngest of four myself. Unfortunately, my older sister, Julia, and I are the only ones left. But we sure did have a blast growing up together. You were guaranteed friends when you had a big family."

"That's true." Vivian laughed. "I do hope having lots of children might be in the cards for our newlyweds here."

"Mom!" Holly lifted her wineglass to her face to hide her blush.

"What?" Vivian's lips shifted into a faux pout. "All I'm saying is you could consider it."

Holly fidgeted with her silverware. "You and Dad only had me."

"Well, we knew to stop at perfection." Vivian rested her elbows on the table and cupped her chin.

"Is that why I'm an only child?" Avery asked, beaming.

Laughter filled the room, with Rachel and Eddie exchanging a look, and the conversation moved to wedding preparations.

Magic was definitely in the mix regarding dinner. Holly couldn't help but indulge. By the time they were done eating and the table was being cleared, she felt like she could only move in slow motion. Despite her stomach weighing her down, the meal had been so good she would do it all again. After managing to rise from her chair, she strolled into the living room to stretch her legs. A walk would definitely provide some relief, but her food coma was making her too sluggish to even consider conquering that feat.

Dasher and Cupid lay on the rug near the Christmas tree, chomping on some doggy treats. Holly gazed at the piece of art on the wall, recalling that Mr. Mason had told her it had been painted by his wife. She could see the brush strokes and imagined the care Mrs. Mason had taken to create just the right aesthetic.

It wasn't until Mr. Mason cleared his throat that she realized he'd come to stand beside her.

"I do the same thing, you know," he said.

"What's that?"

"Find myself staring at it. Of course, in my case, it's because I get swept up in the memory of her smile when she painted. The way splashes of paint would stick to her cheek." He nudged Holly with his elbow. "How she'd tell me I was the best every time I'd bring her tea."

"You do make a pretty good tea."

He chuckled. "So, Holly, I have something for you."

"I didn't know we were exchanging presents tonight. Shouldn't we wait for the others?"

"No, no. This is more of a 'something borrowed' than a Christmas present." He winked and then turned, walking to a side table near the door. He pulled open one of the drawers and took out a wooden box.

Holly's brow wrinkled when he handed it to her.

"It's beautiful." She ran her fingers over the intricately carved design on the top. "What is it?"

Mr. Mason flipped open the lid. "It's a brooch. It belonged to my wife."

The brooch was made of lovely silver and formed in the shape of a curved feather. Set along the shaft of the feather were seven tiny jewels. Holly suspected they were diamonds, but even if they weren't, the brooch was gorgeous.

"It can be placed on clothing or pinned to a veil. My Eleanor wore it to our wedding. And Rachel wore it to hers. You don't have to, so don't feel obligated, but it would mean a lot to me—to Nicky, too, I can imagine—if you were to wear it to yours."

"Mr. Mason. I don't know what to say." Holly had already felt like she was part of the family, but to be included in such a touching tradition solidified it. "I would love that. Thank you."

Nick entered the living room, narrowing his eyes. "Seems like I keep finding you two whispering about something."

Holly turned to face him. "Your dad loaned me your family's brooch to wear on our wedding day." She extended the box.

Nick touched the jewels delicately. "You'll look stunning wearing it. I'm excited to see the whole ensemble put together."

Holly could tell deep thoughts were going on in Nick's mind. That familiar soft look appeared in his eyes whenever he thought about his mother.

Eddie entered the room, carrying a couple of pieces of wood. As he added it to the fireplace, Avery came in and settled between Cupid and Dasher, stroking them both on their heads. Vivian and Rachel chatted about international traveling and planted themselves on the couch.

"I'm going to put this in my purse," Holly whispered to Nick as she closed the brooch box. "I'll be right back."

When she returned, Avery was seated between Rachel and Eddie as Nick updated everyone on the Christmas festival.

"Avery, honey." Rachel rubbed Avery's back. "That's the twelfth time you've yawned in the past half hour. I think it's time for bed."

"No," Avery whined. "It's not fair. You guys always have fun without me."

"That's not true." Eddie kissed the top of her head. "We do tons of stuff with you."

"It's Christmas Eve," Avery argued. "Can I stay up a little longer and open one present?" She held up a finger, her eyes pleading.

"Once you open one, you'll want to open all the others." Rachel laughed.

"No, no, really. Just one," Avery begged.

"No, Avery." Eddie urged her to get up from the couch. "The sooner you go to bed, the earlier you can get up and open *all* your presents."

"You know," Avery said, placing her hands on her hips, "I'm almost ten, which is almost a teenager. And teenagers get to stay up way later than this."

Rachel cringed. "Oh, no, please don't talk about being a teenager yet. I'm not ready."

"Neither of us are," Eddie agreed. "But in any case, Avery, your yawns tell me you need some rest."

Avery turned toward the stairs with a huff. "Fine."

"Tell you what." Nick flashed a smile at her. "You go on and get ready for bed, and I'll come up and say goodnight."

"Or you can come now." Avery tilted her head.

Nick snickered. "Okay, I guess I can come now."

Avery gave him a sheepish grin. "Can Holly come too?"

Nick lifted his brows as he turned to Holly.

"Absolutely, kiddo." Holly held up her hand for a high-five. "Count me in."

Avery slapped Holly's hand. She then kissed her parents and grandfather on the cheek before racing up the stairs ahead of Holly and Nick. She hung a right at the top of the stairs, her arms swinging lazily as she entered her room.

Holly had never been up here before. The ceilings on this floor were high, just like they were on the ground level. Avery's walls were a muted gray-green tone, contrasting nicely with her white furniture. Her bedspread had a lovely pastel floral pattern that gave the room a sense of being alive. In front of a couple of ruffled pillows sat five fluffy stuffed animals. On a small table in the corner stood the dollhouse Nick—ever the brilliant craftsman—had built for Avery.

Avery opened one of her drawers and yanked out some pink, flannel, anime-design pajamas. "I'm just going to change and brush my teeth." She pointed to a rocking chair by the window. "You better call dibs before I get back."

She skipped into the hall and headed toward the bathroom, leaving Holly and Nick staring at each other.

"I don't think I've ever seen her bossy side before," Holly remarked.

Nick laughed. "She definitely knows what she wants."

"That sounds like a Mason trait."

Nick pulled Holly closer. "It's a strong gene."

"Oh, yeah?" Holly rose on her tiptoes and gave him a peck on the lips. "Hey, guess what."

"What?"

She raised a brow, slanting her head toward the rocking chair in the room. "Dibs."

Nick's eyes widened as he chuckled. "Now who's the one going after what she wants?"

Holly batted her lashes as she twirled out of his arms and planted herself in the rocking chair.

Nick groaned in jest as he stuck his fists in his pockets, seemingly accepting defeat.

Whistling a Christmas tune, Avery waltzed into her room, jumped into bed, and tugged the sheets up to her chest. She propped her head on the pillows so that she was slightly sitting up.

Nick sat on the edge of the bed, smoothing the covers. "Did you want us to read you a story?"

"I'm a bit old for that, Uncle Nick. I can read my own books. I'd rather talk."

Nick gave her a sideways look. "What did you want to talk about?"

Avery folded her hands in her lap. "Are you more excited about Christmas or your wedding?"

Holly giggled. "Well, seeing as we're getting married a mere week after Christmas, they pretty much go hand in hand."

"But if you had to pick one?" Avery's mouth twisted into a mischievous grin.

Nick glanced at Holly. She could tell he was holding back a laugh.

"I'd say since Christmas comes around every year," Nick began, "that I'm more excited for our wedding."

Holly flexed her feet to make the rocking chair swing. "My answer is the same."

Avery slid more comfortably into the bed and put her palms behind her head. "Okay, good. That was a test, and you both passed."

Holly and Nick burst into laughter at Avery's snarkiness. With a sobering sigh, Nick got to his feet and leaned over to kiss Avery on her forehead.

"Good night, kiddo."

"Good night, Uncle Nick."

Holly stood. "Sleep tight, Avery."

As she approached the door, Avery sat up.

"Holly," Avery called.

She turned, her hand on the doorframe. "Yeah?"

"I'm glad you're going to be my aunt."

Holly's heart melted. "I am, too."

Avery smiled and lay down again. Holly switched off the light and closed the door behind her.

In the hall, Holly glanced up at Nick and tittered. "So, we passed her test. How do you feel about that?"

"I feel like I could be pretty good at this parenting thing."

"Yeah. One night tucking in your niece and raising a human from a baby to adulthood? Sure, that's the same thing."

Nick hugged her to him. "Are you saying I'm not ready to be a dad?"

Holly ran her hands up his biceps. "On the contrary. I think you're going to be a great father. You definitely have the heart for it."

"And you're going to be an amazing mom."

"No pressure." She sniggered and gave him a quick kiss.

Nick gestured with his head. "As much as I'd like to freeze time and stay like this forever, we'd better go join the others."

"After you."

As they headed downstairs, Holly's thoughts drifted to the

future. They both wanted kids, and her chest flooded with warmth as she imagined the family she and Nick would create together. She wasn't positive they would fulfill her mother's wish of Holly having an abundance of children, but she could imagine two or three little carbon copies of her and Nick completing their unit.

All in good time. First, the wedding.

When they got downstairs, Rachel was serving coffee. Vivian was nowhere to be seen.

Holly scanned the living room, her eyes landing on Eddie. "Do you know where my mom is?"

Eddie poked the fire and regarded Holly over his shoulder. "She's out on the deck."

"What? But it's freezing out."

Eddie set down the poker and stood. "I think she wanted to watch the snow."

Holly nodded and grabbed a throw blanket from the couch before heading toward the back door. As soon as she opened the door, Dasher and Cupid darted out, eager to play in the thick snow. Flurries drifted around her, and the moon illuminated the night sky. She wrapped herself in the blanket and approached her mom, who stood at the edge of the deck, resting her elbows on the railing and gazing out onto Rachel and Eddie's backyard. Vivian let out a giggle as Cupid and Dasher playfully pounced on one another, kicking up flakes into their fur.

Vivian continued staring into the distance. "It's beautiful, isn't it?"

Holly draped one end of the blanket over her mother's shoulders. "You know you can watch the snow fall from inside."

"I like the full immersive experience." Vivian laughed. "Besides, it reminds me of your father."

Though Holly's skin tingled from the cold, she was warmed by a sense of calm that came over her. "Yeah. Me too."

"I can remember the first time he brought me to Silverwood. I had never seen snow before, at least not in person. But movies and TV shows can't prepare you for the magic of your first snowfall. Of the first time a tiny, cold snowflake drifts onto your cheek, melts, and becomes a part of your soul."

"It's hard for me to imagine growing up without having experienced snow."

Vivian set a hand on Holly's. "Because we brought you here every year since you were a baby. Silverwood has always been a part of *your* soul."

Holly smiled and leaned her head against her mom's temple. "Thank you for that."

"Your father wouldn't have had it any other way." Vivian's body shook as she chuckled. "He loved Silverwood. Loved being out in the snow. Hiking, sledding, snowball fights. He never did have the knack for skiing, though."

"Is that why we never went?"

"Well, I was no good at it, either. I could climb a banana tree in my bare feet back then, but I couldn't stay upright on skis for the life of me."

"It's a good thing my friends and I took lessons in high school, then."

Dasher ducked his head into the snow while Cupid bounced in a circle around him, barking.

"Most of all," Vivian continued, "your father loved Christmas. Loved everything about it, especially the Silverwood Christmas market. That's why he built that sled."

"Sleigh, Mom."

"That's what I said." Vivian snickered, obviously knowing she'd said the wrong word but being stubborn about it. "He put all his love for Christmas into that sleigh. I know he would be so happy and proud that you made it part of the annual Christmas celebration."

Holly snaked her arm around her mother and squeezed her tightly. "I'm glad you think so, Mom. I think he would, too."

Chapter Eighteen

The mountain was blanketed in white. The sky could've been bluer, but Viola didn't mind. She breathed in the crisp, cold air and reveled in the fact that she was going skiing today. For someone who lived in a mountain town, she didn't ski nearly as much as she would have liked.

Silverwood Sky wasn't overly crowded today, but plenty of people were in attendance. Knowing the children's charity would receive a nice donation from the lift tickets warmed Viola's heart.

Viola waited as Jonas clipped into his skis. He fumbled a bit, holding his helmet and goggles in one hand while trying to line one runner parallel with the other. She held back a laugh as she went to help him.

She wanted to put her arms around him to hold him steady but resisted the urge.

This isn't a date, remember? It's platonic. No matter how cute he is.

"Here, put this on first." Viola took his helmet from his hand and hovered it over his head.

Jonas pulled down the headgear and secured the strap. Viola wrapped the goggles over the helmet but kept them up near his forehead for now.

"This seems like a lot of effort," Jonas complained.

"Stop being a baby. This is for your safety."

"So you're saying this is dangerous." Jonas squinted as he looked up at the mountain. "Maybe we shouldn't be doing this."

"I thought you said you've been skiing before."

"I have." He shrugged. "Once. Admittedly, it was years ago. And now I recall why there wasn't a second time."

Viola set his skis straight and tapped his knee, indicating he should stick his boot into the notch. "We're not going on the expert slope, but still, you don't want to crush your skull running into a tree or anything."

"You're not making me feel better about this." He lifted his legs to check if his skis were secure.

Viola led the way to the ski lift, breathing in the cool mountain air. Her pulse raced, and she embraced the rush of adrenaline.

They got in line for the lift, and Viola couldn't help but notice Jonas fidgeting with his ski poles.

"Isn't there a storm headed this way?" he asked.

"Not anymore. It took an unexpected turn. We're good to go. Just look at that sky."

Jonas crinkled his nose as he looked skyward. "Those, uh, lifts seem to be moving pretty fast, don't you think?"

Viola studied the speed of the seats hanging on the moving cable. "Doesn't seem to be unusually speedy, no."

"Are they shaking? I think they might be wobbling or something. When's the last time they were inspected?"

"Quit playing around. Are you ready?" Viola asked.

Jonas adjusted his gloves, staring at the approaching lift chairs. "Yeah. Sure. Um, Yeah."

"What's wrong?"

"Nothing?" He blew out a quick breath.

Viola had to smirk. "Are you scared?"

"Me? No. Scared?" He cleared his throat. "How, uh, how safe are those wires? Do you know how often they are tested?"

"Jonas Brickman, are you afraid of heights?"

"Heights?" He forced a chuckle. "No. No. I'm not, uh … It's not the height. It's the falling I'm concerned about."

"You're not going to fall."

"You can guarantee that?"

"How about this? Once we're on the lift, I'll hold your hand. That way, if you fall, we both fall."

"Why would you think that would make me feel better?"

"So you don't want to hold my hand?"

"Well, yeah. I will take you up on that offer. But I still don't think you understand how gravity works."

She bit her cheek. "Okay. I'll distract you with some lovely conversation."

His gaze was still glued to the moving cable. "I suppose we could give it a try."

"Good. Let's go."

Because of the height of the mountain, the line progressed relatively quickly.

"All right, hold your poles close to you," Viola instructed. "But don't put your hands through the straps."

They scooted forward onto the lifting area. Viola stood on the marked line and told Jonas to do the same. He blew out a long breath as the chair came toward them.

"Since you're sitting on that side, hold your poles in your right hand." Viola spoke sweetly, trying not to overwhelm him. "And look over your left shoulder, bend your knees, and sit when the seat hits the back of your legs. Here we go."

Viola reached back as the chair contacted them. She pulled at the bar, so it was secure in front of them.

"Okay, sit back and no rocking," she said.

"Oh, believe me. I may be shaking in fear, but there's no way I'll intentionally rock this thing."

She watched his eyes dart around as the bench elevated off the ground. When he visibly swallowed, she almost giggled. She couldn't help but notice how cute he looked, even if his expression was full of terror.

"Now we just look for the signs."

Jonas cleared his throat. "Aren't you supposed to be distracting me?"

"Sorry. Right." She took his hand in hers. "Look how beautiful the mountain is."

"Looking at the object I don't want to fall to my death on isn't actually helping."

She chuckled. "Okay, okay." Her mind raced to come up with something else to distract him. Without thinking, she blurted out the first thing that came to her. "So tell me about Lacey."

He blinked, a crease forming between his brows. "How do you know about Lacey?"

Dread ran through her. She forced herself to keep the smile on her face. "Is that your girlfriend?"

Despite his anxiety, he laughed. "No. LACEE is a business investment. It stands for Logistic Associates Cyber Engineering Enterprises. LACEE for short."

Viola felt as if a weight had dropped from her shoulders. A quiver stirred in her stomach. "I see. Well, you can see why that could be confusing."

"I suppose. But where did you hear the name?"

She cringed. "It was when I broke that vase at the manor. Accidentally. And, uh, me overhearing that part of your conversation was *also* an accident."

"So you thought I was involved with some woman back in Billings."

She gave him a half-shrug. "Yeah."

"And that bothered you?"

She narrowed her eyes. "I didn't say that. You're awfully presumptuous. Kind of like how you presume I'm going to wait for you when we reach the top of the mountain."

"Hey, come on. That's not fair."

"All right." She raised her chin. "I'll wait for you, but we never mention the vase, the opened letter, or the eavesdropping again."

He arched a brow. "I'm not used to this."

"What?"

"Not being in charge of a negotiation."

Viola snickered. "Do we have a deal or not?"

Jonas gave her a sideways grin. "Deal."

"See, it worked."

"What worked?"

Viola shrugged. "Us chatting. I kept your mind off your fear of heights, right?"

He snickered. "Until now, anyway. Thanks for bringing it up."

"Don't worry. We're about to get off." She pointed to the sign that told them to raise the bar and prepare to unload.

"Hmm, I think I'm still going to need your assistance."

She squeezed his hand. "I'm here for you."

Viola elevated the bar, and Jonas let out a shuddered breath.

"Okay, point the tips of your skis upward." She released his hand and adjusted her position. "When our skis are touching the ground completely, lean forward. The chair will give us a little push. We don't want it knocking us over, so straighten your body and go with it."

Despite finding humor in how anxious he was, she was nervous for him. She gestured for him to follow her lead. In a matter of moments, she guided him off the lift and out of the way of the other dismounting skiers.

"Better?" Her smile was wide. Though she doubted he would

have plummeted to his death, she was glad they'd arrived at the peak in one piece.

"Now that I'm touching the ground? Yes." Moving his skis with exaggerated knee lifts, he shifted to face her. "Now it's just a question of—Whoa!"

He'd turned at the wrong angle and began drifting backward down the slope. Viola's eyes widened. She stretched her arms out in a futile attempt to catch him. It was too late. He was sliding farther and farther away.

Viola pulled her goggles over her eyes and pushed off with her poles. He wasn't too far, but she could tell he was worried by the look on his face. She caught up to him and shifted to the side, hoping to bring her skis in front of him to stop his momentum. Instead, their runners got tangled, and they both toppled to the ground. Snow kicked up into their faces, and it took a moment before Viola could figure out if all arms and legs were intact.

"Are you all right?" he asked, reaching for her arm to help her sit up.

"Are you?"

His breath came out in spurts as he glanced around. "Yeah. I think so. Just a little embarrassed."

After a second of assessing the situation, Viola couldn't hold back her laughter anymore. Her lungs hurt from the frigid air she sucked in, but she couldn't stop.

"Hey, it's not funny," Jonas said, but he was smiling. A few seconds later, his laughs joined hers.

"I hope nobody filmed that," Viola said once her giggles had subsided. "That's not exactly how I'd like to go viral."

"Agreed." Jonas managed to get to his feet.

He'd lost a ski but reached out to pull Viola up before hunting it down. The minute they were settled, she gazed at him.

"Are you ready to head down?" she asked.

"Is it all right if we go slow?"

"As slow as the mountain allows, sure."

"I just have to warn you." He shook his head. "I can't promise I'll be going up that lift again, so this might be our only trip down the mountain."

"Oh, I don't know. The ride down might be worth the trip up. You'll see. Most of the time, the harder you work to achieve something, the more you appreciate it in the end."

His gaze trailed over her features. His expression was so intense that Viola's breath left her momentarily. Now, she was the one who was afraid of falling.

"That is true." He lowered the goggles over his eyes. "Well, then. Let's conquer this mountain."

Chapter Nineteen

Luckily, the initial tumble Viola and Jonas had taken was the only hiccup they'd encountered. Viola was proud of herself for convincing Jonas to travel up the ski lift a few more times before the dark clouds shambled in. The unexpected change of weather meant they had to cut their excursion short, and as they made their way back to the chateau, the conditions only got worse.

Gathering her things from the chateau kitchen, she texted her mother.

> Viola: Mom, I'm on my way. You okay?

> Mom: It's really bad out there. I heard a crash outside. Oliver is here and checking on it.

> Viola: He should just wait until the storm is over. Hang tight. I'll be home soon.

> Mom: Be careful. I heard on the news that it's coming in full force.

> Viola: I will.

She flung the strap of her duffel bag over her shoulder and marched to the front door of the building, determined to get through the storm and be with her mother. At least Oliver was there, but she didn't know how long he could stay.

She yanked open the door and stepped outside. An ice-cold blanket of freezing air and snow struck her in the face. Viola shielded her eyes, but all she could see was heavy snowfall pelting the parking lot. How had it escalated so quickly?

She forced herself to go down the veranda stairs and took slow steps toward where she believed her car was parked, but the powerful wind drove her back, almost knocking her over.

"Are you crazy?" Jonas's voice was loud behind her. "Get back inside."

"I need to get to my mom. I have to make sure she's all right."

"You'll never make it past the parking lot." He placed his hands on her shoulders and urged her to return indoors. "Come on. You can call to make sure she's safe, but I can't let you drive in this. It's way too dangerous."

A heavy feeling settled in her chest. She didn't want to abandon her mother, but Jonas was right. Reluctantly, she pivoted and followed him inside.

Even with the doors closed, the stormy winds were deafening. Viola shivered, wiping the wet snow out of her face. She pulled out her phone and pushed the contact button for her mother.

"Viola, I was just about to call you."

Viola could feel her pulse pounding in her ears. "Mom, is everything all right? Did something happen?"

"No. But Oliver said the roads are a mess. He's stuck here. Which means you shouldn't be driving, either."

"You're right. I know. I'm at the Lakeside Chateau. I'll stay here until the storm dies down."

"Yes, please. I don't want you out there in this."

"Okay." Viola turned toward Jonas, who dug a flashlight out of a drawer. "Stay away from the windows. Keep warm. I'll call you soon." She blew out a breath and slipped her device back into her coat pocket. "Now what?"

Jonas tested the flashlight. Viola breathed a sigh of relief when it worked.

"Now we wait," he answered.

She drew nearer to Jonas. "I love everything about Silverwood except the storms."

"The town is still standing despite its onslaught of harsh weather. I think it'll survive this one too. We'll probably lose power." He held up the flashlight. "In any case, we're safer here than we'd be out there."

As she was about to search for a comfortable place to sit out the storm, they were plunged into darkness. Viola gasped, her heart pounding in her throat. She reached out, and when she found Jonas's arm, he pulled her closer. She unintentionally dug her fingers into his biceps.

"It's all right," he reassured her. "Like I predicted, the storm cut the power."

She nodded against his shoulder.

Jonas switched on the flashlight. "Are you okay?"

She realized she'd been clenching his shirt, her grip firm on the material. Hesitantly, she eased up on her hold. "Yeah. Sorry. I just got frightened."

The wind howled and whistled in the building, sounding like a train barreling toward them. A crash resonated, and Viola jumped.

"I think a tree branch might have broken a window. At least, I hope it's just a branch." He released her, the beam of his light aimed at the stairs. "I'm going to check it out."

Viola struggled to pull out her phone. She turned on the device's flashlight and followed Jonas.

"Wait." She swallowed hard. "I'll go with you."

Viola stuck close to Jonas as they traveled through the building. A cold gust of wind snaked around her. They tracked the whistling sound to locate the source of the breach.

They arrived at a conference room near Jonas's office. Shattered glass littered the carpet. The blinds rattled, and a tree branch protruded through the broken windowpane.

Viola's hair whipped about her face as she watched Jonas inspect the damage.

"Was that from the Christmas tree out front?" she asked.

"Looks like it."

He reached for the branch.

"You'll cut yourself," she called out.

The warning didn't stop him. He wrenched the branch free and then forced it out through the opening in the glass. Squinting against the stormy gales, he inspected his hand. When he mumbled a curse, Viola knew he'd been injured.

"Do you have a first aid kit?" she asked.

"In my office."

They hurried to his office, where Jonas dragged a case out of a cabinet. At first, he attempted to tend to his wound himself, which proved impossible.

"Here." Viola took the bandage from him. "Let me help."

They sat on his leather couch while she wrapped his injury, the room quiet as she worked. He aimed the flashlight so she could see what she was doing. With the bright beam practically in her eyes, she couldn't be certain where his focus was, but she sensed he was staring at her.

"Does that feel tight enough?" she asked once she'd secured the bandage.

He flexed his fingers. "Yes. Thanks. We need to find something to cover the hole in the window. The carpet is already soaked, and that snow's just going to keep coming in."

Viola forced the wheels in her head to spin. "The oven trays are big. They should work."

"Good idea." He stood. "I've got some duct tape in the supply closet. Should hold for now. You think you could get the trays and meet me back here?"

She didn't want to split up, but she knew the job would get done faster if they did. Standing, she feigned confidence. "Sounds like a plan."

Jonas faced her and placed his hands on her shoulders. "It'll be all right. We can do this. We conquered a mountain. Now, we have to conquer the storm."

Viola nodded, swallowing so hard she could barely breathe. Jonas squeezed her shoulders before heading out the office door.

It'll be fine. Just like he said. I simply have to go to the kitchen and grab a couple of trays. Easy peasy.

She gulped down a breath and moved out to the hall. Aiming her phone's flashlight with one hand and gripping the wall with the other, Viola headed to the kitchen. She flinched at the scraping sounds emanating from somewhere in the building.

It's branches pitching against the outside wall. That's all. Get it together.

By the time she got to the kitchen, her leg muscles felt too tense. The wind howled through the exhaust vents. Despite the shakiness in her limbs, she told herself to grab what was necessary and go. The hinges of the industrial oven squeaked as she opened it. After grabbing two trays, she darted out of the kitchen without bothering to close the oven door.

The sense of urgency escalated as she ran back to Jonas. She knew she was being ridiculous; there'd been plenty of winter storms in Silverwood—at least one each season—and she'd survived them all. But there was something sinister about this one that spiked her adrenaline.

When she reached the office, her stomach felt heavy, as if it were filled with rocks. Dizziness threw her off-balance, and it wasn't until Jonas caught her that she realized she'd almost collapsed.

"Hey, are you all right?" he asked.

She squeezed her eyes and held her palms to her temples. "I-I just got dizzy for a moment."

"We haven't eaten anything all day." He picked up everything she had dropped. "Let's repair the damage, and then we can find something to eat."

"Yeah. There's food in the kitchen."

"Perfect. One step at a time, okay?"

She bowed her head. "Okay."

They worked together to fix the window, with Viola holding the trays in place as Jonas performed some duct tape magic. Once the barrier was secure, they backed up and stared at their work.

"I think that should do it," Jonas said.

Viola swayed.

"Hey, hey." He wrapped his arm around her to support her weight. "Don't give out on me. Let's go to the kitchen and get some food in you."

"Yes. Let's do that."

Viola felt a sense of security in his arms as he helped her down the stairs and to the kitchen. He found a chair for her and then used his flashlight to search the industrial refrigerator.

"Look." He aimed the light at his face so she could see his smile. "There's still pie."

"Are you okay, Mom? Do you need anything?" Holly handed her mom a blanket.

Vivian placed it on her bed. "I'm fine. I know all about the

Silverwood storms. And besides, I lived through many typhoons in the Philippines."

"Okay, I'm going to help Nick get Cupid out from under the sideboard. He crawled under there when the wind picked up, and getting him out is impossible."

"Good luck. And don't worry about me. I'll be fine. I have a book. And a flashlight in case the power goes out."

"All right. I'll check in on you later." Holly made her way to the dining room.

"Come on, Cupid." Nick had crouched beside the sideboard.

"I'm not used to seeing him scared." Holly sat cross-legged on the floor. Though the scream of the wind unnerved her, she chose to concentrate on the frightened Malamute. "He braved last year's storm."

"This one is worse. Or maybe he's not feeling well."

"What can we do to calm him?"

Nick straightened and scrubbed his jaw. "When he was a puppy and had trouble sleeping, I would play my guitar."

Holly's eyes widened slightly. "I love that idea."

"I don't know." He grimaced. "I'm a little rusty."

"Makes sense. We've been together for a year, and I've yet to hear you play. You even brought it over months ago, intending to play it, but it hasn't happened."

"Well, if you think it will help, then tonight could be my comeback."

"I do think it will help." Holly playfully batted her lashes. "Come on. Do it for Cupid."

Nick left to retrieve his guitar.

Holly shifted until she was on all fours. Bending her head toward the floor, she called out to Cupid, "Hey, brave boy. You're all right." She reached under the sideboard and stroked the whimpering dog's forehead.

She'd never seen him like this, and part of her wondered if it was more than just the storm. Hopefully, he wasn't sick. Holly pressed her cheek to the hardwood and scooted closer, petting his neck.

"Now I've got to get both of you out of there," Nick joked from above her.

Holly backed out of the crawlspace and rested with her head against the sideboard.

Nick strummed the guitar once. "It's out of tune."

Holly watched as he twisted the pegs at the guitar's neck. When each string was properly tuned, he joined Holly on the floor and began to play.

She wasn't familiar with the melody but felt it encompassing her soul like a warm blanket. She found herself staring at Nick as his fingers moved effortlessly over the strings, the music he made infusing tranquility into an otherwise tense situation.

After a couple of verses, Cupid shuffled forward, poking his head out from beneath the sideboard.

Nick glanced at Holly as he continued to strum, and she gazed at him like a groupie.

Cupid whined again but emerged completely, resting his head on Nick's leg. When the song ended, Nick gently placed his guitar beside him and stroked Cupid's head. He regarded Holly, finding her eyes locked with his.

"What?" he asked.

"I feel like the luckiest woman alive."

She shifted so she could get nearer and kissed him tenderly.

Cupid rotated and stretched out his paw to Holly.

"Let's elope," she suddenly said.

Nick bent his neck to search her face, his brows knitted together. "What?"

She sighed. "Let's just do it. Elope and forget all this crazy planning."

"What brought this on?"

She shrugged. "I don't know. I guess I just want to marry you. Is having a big party really worth all the stress?"

Nick took her hand. "I didn't realize you were so stressed. Let me help you. Because I'm pretty sure your mother would have some words if you suddenly canceled the party she flew halfway across the world to attend."

"I think she'd be fine." It sounded more like a question than a statement. Holly felt she couldn't look him in the eyes.

"Okay, there's something you're not telling me." He lifted her chin. "What's going on?"

Holly bit her lip. "It's probably nothing, but Kim told me Grayson threatened to ruin our wedding. And while I know it was probably an empty threat, I've had this feeling like someone's been watching me. My common sense tells me I'm imagining it, but it's making me panic a little. But if there's a small chance he really is out to get us, and we eloped, there would be no wedding for him to ruin."

Nick was silent, seemingly taking in her words. Ice pelted the windows, resounding through the silence in the house.

"Holly, why didn't you tell me about this before?"

Holly fidgeted with the sleeve of her sweater. "I didn't want to dampen your spirits with something that might not be true. I suppose I wanted to spare you from unpleasant notions of Grayson and his possible evil plan, especially if it's just something I'm imagining."

Nick smirked. "First of all, if anything is ever burdening you, I want you to tell me. One of my jobs as your fiancé is to be a shoulder to lean on. Secondly, if your deepest wish is for us to elope right now, I wouldn't hesitate. There's nothing more I want than to be married to you, but I don't want to do it just because your ex may or may not be out to ruin the big day. I'm not afraid of him, and I won't allow him to hurt you in any way."

As Nick's words washed over her, a comforting warmth blossomed in her chest, radiating through her veins like a gentle embrace. It was as if a weight had been lifted from her shoulders, replaced by a profound sense of security and reassurance. Her heartbeat steadied, and a newfound strength coursed within her.

She cupped his face and placed a tender kiss on his lips. "Thank you. You always know the perfect thing to say."

Cupid raised his head and yawned, causing the couple to laugh.

With a sigh, Holly petted Cupid, settling next to Nick to wait out the storm.

Chapter Twenty

Holly stretched and swung her legs over the bed. After slipping her feet into a pair of fuzzy slippers, she trudged toward the kitchen. Her head was calling for coffee after a night of little sleep. The storm had eventually died down, but Holly's adrenaline had taken longer to dwindle.

Before she reached the kitchen, she found Nick in the living room, pulling on his boots.

"Good morning." Holly kissed him on the cheek.

Cupid sniffed her slippers and then looked up at her curiously, his tongue hanging out as he panted.

"Good morning," Nick replied.

"Where are you off to?"

"I thought Cupid could use some fresh air after last night." Nick grabbed a tennis ball off the table. "We're going for a run up the mountain to toss the ball around a bit before I have to go to work."

"It snowed a lot. Be careful on the roads."

"We will." Nick pulled on his coat.

Holly tilted her head. "Will Cupid be able to find the ball in all that snow?"

"He loves a challenge."

"I think he gets that from you." Holly fixed his dark gray scarf and then used it to pull him in for a kiss. "Have you seen my mom yet?"

"No. I think she's still asleep."

"Ah, okay, I'll let her sleep in a bit. That wind was so loud, it echoed in my dreams."

Nick pocketed the tennis ball. "Hopefully, the worst is over."

She smiled at him. "Have fun on the mountain."

"See you later."

When Nick and Cupid left, all was quiet. Holly went into the kitchen, grateful the coffee had already been brewed. She poured a steaming cup and had just made her way to her laptop on the kitchen table when her phone buzzed.

"Hello?"

"Ms. St. Ives, it's Marie from Blossom Boutique."

Holly tensed. Something was wrong. "Yes?"

"I'm afraid I have some terrible news."

She shook. Though Nick's reassuring words had calmed her the night before, her nerves became frazzled all over again. "What is it?"

"The shop suffered considerable damage because of the storm." Marie's voice cracked as if she were holding back tears. "The front window was completely broken in from branches flying free in the wind. That let the snow in, and we don't know if that had anything to do with the electrical fire or ..." She trailed off and sniffled.

"Oh, no. I'm so sorry."

There was another sniffle on the line. "Eighty percent of our stock is ruined. Including your gown, I'm afraid."

Holly couldn't find her breath. Was this really happening? Marie continued to speak, but Holly could barely process anything she was saying.

"I'm so sorry this happened to you," Holly said. "This must be so heartbreaking. I hope your insurance covers the damages."

"I hope so, too. And I'm sorry about your dress. I know your wedding is coming up in a few days."

In four days, to be exact.

"Yeah, um … is there anything I can do?" Holly asked her. "Can I get another dress?"

"I've contacted the distributor, asking if the stock could be delivered to my home for the time being—you know, until I can get the shop renovated. But it would take at least a week for the shipment to arrive. I'm so sorry. I can offer you a refund."

Whatever Marie said after that was lost in the buzz of Holly's oncoming migraine. The next thing she knew, she was sitting on the couch with her head between her hands, staring at the floor.

She thought about calling Nick to tell him what had happened but couldn't bring herself to say the words. Holly had fallen in love with the gown she'd picked out. She was thankful her bridal party had taken their dresses home already. At least there was that. Still, her heart felt as if it were in a vise.

She was barely aware of her mother coming out of her room and studying her.

"Holly, is everything all right?"

Holly gaped at her mother. She opened her mouth to speak, but her vocal cords weren't cooperating.

Vivian's brow furrowed as she hurried to sit next to her daughter. She put an arm around her and rubbed her back. "Oh, baby. Don't worry. Whatever it is, we can work through it." She laughed. "Actually, my father—your *lolo*—used to say that to me, but he meant *work* as in actual physical labor. He said you'd be too exhausted to worry about your problem by the time you were done."

Holly swiped her hair away from her face. "I guess that's one way of coping."

"More like avoiding." Vivian smoothed down Holly's strands. "Tell me what happened."

"The dress shop called. The storm knocked out a window and somehow started a fire. They think it was electrical. But the shop and everything in it was destroyed."

Vivian's eyes widened. "Your gown?"

Holly burst into tears. "My gown."

Vivian embraced her as Holly cried on her shoulder. She held Holly, slowly rocking.

"I can't believe this is happening. First, my caterer, then Nick's father has to go to the hospital, and now this. What am I going to do?"

"First of all, I'm very sorry this happened. That poor shop owner. What a tragedy."

Holly nodded. "Yes, I feel so bad for her. That was her livelihood."

"Secondly, you could wear a potato sack and still be the most beautiful bride there ever was. And probably make potato sacks trendy in the process."

Holly snorted through her tears.

"And third, you have a backup dress that looks stunning on you."

Holly lifted her head from her mother's shoulder and wiped the wetness from her cheeks. "Right." She sniffled. "The dress Auntie Seng made."

"Good thing I brought it, right?"

Holly nodded, sniffling again. "Thank you, Mom."

"Of course, my darling. Oftentimes, the harder it is for things to turn out how we want, the more we appreciate what we get instead." Vivian kissed her temple. "As a side note, Nick's father is doing fine."

"I know. That's true."

Between defeat and exhaustion, Holly recognized a glimpse of hope. She embraced her mother and prayed the worst was behind her.

Chapter Twenty-One

"Thank you, Oliver." Viola handed him cash. "There's no way I could have set this up myself."

"You're welcome." Oliver pocketed the money. "You got it from here?"

Viola admired the evergreen. "Absolutely. It just needs decorating now. Go on. Don't keep your girlfriend waiting."

"All right." He waved. "I'll see you. Have fun."

Oliver headed toward his car, leaving Viola on the veranda of the Lakeside Chateau. She'd caught a lucky break when Nick had told her there was one tree left from his farm that was the size she needed. She'd lucked out again when Oliver had said he was free to help her stand it up in front of the building.

Viola removed the lid from the container she'd brought and dug out a shiny bauble. When the storm had destroyed the Christmas tree at the venue's entrance, Viola had suggested Jonas replace it. He had, of course, replied that there was no need since Christmas was over anyway, brushing it off as unimportant. But Viola had insisted that New Year's Eve wasn't complete without a Christmas tree and that people coming to the venue would expect to see one. When he'd contended that it probably wasn't possible to find a tree since Christmas was over, his pessimism sparked an obstinate determination in Viola to prove him wrong. Jonas hadn't believed she could find one, but he'd underestimated her. As she crouched to grab the string of lights from the box, she grinned, imagining the look on

Jonas's face when he saw the New Year's miracle she'd pulled off.

Too excited about her project to be bothered by the cold, Viola managed to string the lights and hang the garland before Jonas showed up.

"What are you doing?" Jonas sauntered up the exterior steps of the building.

She smirked. "You said I could set it up if I found a big enough tree."

He scoffed and shook his head. "How did you find one after Christmas?"

"I have connections." She raised her brows. "Well, don't just stand there. Help me decorate it."

"What? Me?" He came nearer, hands in his coat pockets. "No. I, uh, I don't really enjoy the whole decorating thing."

"Oh, right. You're the not-so-into-Christmas guy." Viola shrugged. "Suit yourself."

Since he was still watching, she purposely clustered several baubles on one branch, weighing it down.

"That doesn't, uh … that's not how you do it." He gestured at the branch, a subtle flicker of scrutiny passing across his features.

She played dumb. "What do you mean? It looks great."

"No. You're supposed to spread them out more." He approached the tree and rearranged the ornaments. "This is just sloppy."

Viola bit her cheek. "I see."

She hung a few more baubles on the same branch.

Jonas clicked his tongue and moved them elsewhere. "No. Like this."

She laughed.

He squinted. "Did you just manipulate me?"

"I knew you were too much of a control freak to let that go."

"Control freak?" He sounded exasperated, but amusement

danced in his eyes. "I'll have you know I'm perfectly capable of letting things get out of control. When I feel like it."

"You? Come on."

He scoffed. In the next second, he scooped a handful of snow off the veranda railing, packed it up, and whipped it in her direction.

She ducked, but the snowball still pelted her in the shoulder.

"Now you've started it." She retaliated quickly, not caring that the snow was freezing her gloveless hands.

Her snowball hit him in the chest, but he'd already hurled another her way.

She bobbed, making her way down the stairs. She needed more ammunition, and the ground was covered with it.

Dodging heavy snowballs, Jonas hurried down the stairs and dove to the ground. He rapidly got to his feet, but his cashmere coat was marked with white flakes.

She crouched to gather more snow, but before she could track him, Jonas charged, and frosty flakes splattered all over her face. As she blinked the white powder out of her eyes, he caught her by the waist with both arms and slammed into her, driving her backward. They landed in a blanket of thick snow with Jonas on top.

Viola mustered enough energy to grab a fresh handful and smash it into Jonas's hair. He rolled off her, letting out a gasp. When he brushed the snow out of his mane, Viola laughed. Of course he would be worried about his hair in a moment like this.

He narrowed his eyes, but there was still a dazzling grin on his face. "What?"

She sat up. "I got you."

As his eyes roamed over her features, she sobered, getting lost in his stare.

"Yeah," he responded softly. "You did."

He reached toward her, but she didn't flinch. Something about the way he looked at her caused a flutter in her stomach. He pushed away a strand of hair that had clung to her cheek.

Was he leaning in closer?

"Mr. Brickman, I'm sorry to interrupt."

Viola looked past him to see Susan standing near the barely decorated Christmas tree. Her red coat was open, which implied Susan wouldn't stay outside one minute longer than she had to.

"It's Billings on the line," Susan said. "They said they couldn't reach you on your cell."

Jonas cleared his throat as he jumped up. "Thank you. I'll be right there."

Susan nodded and headed back into the building, rubbing her arms.

Jonas straightened his coat and held out a hand to Viola. For some reason, she felt a tightness in her chest. All at once, the cold was unbearable. Was she disappointed that the moment had passed? What had it even meant? It had just been a playful snowball fight. But if that were true, why did her stomach feel like it was tied up in knots at the thought of him leaving?

She took his hand and allowed him to pull her to her feet.

"I need to take this call." He brushed the white powder off his coat. "Not sure how long it will be, but I'll try to hurry back and help you finish the decorations."

She moved her hair away from her cheeks. "Don't even worry about it. Go take care of business."

His smile was timid and gone in a flash as he turned and strolled into the chateau.

Viola watched him go, brushing stray snowflakes from her hair. A cool breeze rushed by, and she stretched her neck, taking in the enormous structure of the building and the massive sky above it. Twinkling stars stared back at her. She followed the panorama down to the snow-covered mountains in the distance. Moonlight reflected on the lake. She could just make out the glass-enclosed winter garden where Holly and Nick's ceremony would take place. Their wedding arch already stood there, minus the fresh flowers.

Jonas certainly has a beautiful building.

She supposed he had to be tenacious with his business to keep everything running professionally. He was a busy man, and Viola wasn't positive there was room in his life for her.

Her gaze went back to the tree. Somehow, she doubted he would be back anytime soon. With a sigh, she resolved to finish decorating alone.

Chapter Twenty-Two

Holly smoothed down her dress and triple-checked her hair in the mirror. She wasn't even sure what went on at a bachelorette party anymore. All she knew was that Kim had told her she'd take care of everything and that Holly should wear her little black dress and be ready to dance.

"You look nice." Vivian appeared in the doorway.

"Thanks, Mom. So do you."

Vivian did a twirl in her yellow outfit. "I haven't been out dancing in a long time. I wonder if I've got any moves left."

"If it makes you feel any better, I don't know if I've got any moves, either."

A car horn caused them both to turn.

"Is that her?" Holly furrowed her brow. "Does she want us to get in her Uber or …"

Holly went to the living room window and pushed the curtain aside. Her jaw dropped when she spotted the white stretch limousine idling in front of the cabin. Two seconds later, Kim appeared through the limo's sunroof, holding a glass of champagne.

Holly laughed. "I should have known."

When she turned around, Vivian was putting on her winter jacket.

"She hired a limo," Holly announced as she fetched her coat.

"Typical Kim." Vivian chuckled. "I guess we're partying New York style."

After Holly locked the door behind them, she and her mom made their way to the vehicle through the snow. Kim let out a *whoop* so loud that Holly was afraid Mrs. Miranelli would be able to hear her from down the street.

"Hey, Holly-bear," Kim called. "Get in so we can start this par-tay."

When Holly opened the rear side door, she was welcomed by a chorus of "Surprise!" Lucy and Rachel sat in the lush interior, the former toasting Holly with a glass of bubbly and the latter snacking on pretzels.

"This is great," Holly said as Kim came in from the sunroof. "Where's Emily?"

"She said sorry she can't make it. Her arthritis is acting up, and she doesn't think she can stay up all night like she used to." Kim grabbed a handful of nuts from the limo bar. "She sends her love, though."

Once they were settled, Kim and Lucy started singing along to a current pop song while Rachel and Vivian danced in their seats. Holly swung her foot to the beat, laughing and smiling so much her cheeks hurt.

"Okay, okay." Kim raised her hands, calling for everyone's attention. "I have something for everyone here."

"Oh, this ought to be good," Vivian joked.

Kim snickered as she pulled a large gift bag from under the seat. The first item she extracted was a silky, ivory sash. Across it, written in gold, were the words "Bride-to-be."

"For you, milady." Kim held the sash open above Holly's head.

Holly slipped it on over her coat, giggling at how ridiculous she must have looked. Lucy wolf-whistled at her.

"I've got one for each of us," Kim announced, reaching into the bag again.

The sashes she produced for herself and Lucy were marked with the word "Bridesmaid." Vivian's said, "Mother of the Bride," and Rachel's, "Maid of Honor."

"I know, I know." Kim flailed her hands around. "It should say '*Matron* of Honor,' but I wasn't as brushed up as Holly on all the correct technical terms, so—"

"No, it's great." Rachel smiled as she adjusted her sash so the title could be read. "Thank you."

"And just so Holly feels extra special …" Kim removed a gold tiara from the bag and made a big show of it. Holly gasped, and the rest of the gang gave exaggerated *ooh*s and *ahh*s before bursting into fits of laughter.

The singing and dancing continued, and a few songs later, Holly glanced out the window. She recognized the street they were on.

"Are we going to Le Ruban Rouge?" Holly swiveled to face Kim.

"You didn't think I'd forget to include food in this event, did you?" Kim took a sip of her champagne. "Lucky for us, Rachel told me about your favorite restaurant in Silverwood."

"And lucky for me," Lucy added, "it's my favorite, too."

"First dinner," Kim said as she raised her glass, "then dancing."

Lucy, Kim, and Holly *whooped* and hollered. Rachel snapped photos with her phone.

Vivian chuckled. "All right, girls. If we don't settle down, they won't let us into *any* restaurant."

The singing and giggling became a little tamer as the limo came to a halt. The group climbed out of the vehicle, which took up three parking spaces, and strode toward the restaurant entrance. The excitement of the evening's festivities coursed through Holly's veins, kindling a warmth within her despite the chilly weather. And it had only just begun.

They entered the establishment, and Holly followed Rachel to the greeter at the front of the restaurant. The podium she stood behind was decorated in evergreens and red velvet bows. While they were shown to their table, Holly politely nodded and smiled at familiar people she passed. The greeter took them to an L-shaped staircase leading to an upper floor. Twinkling lights hung along the railing and around pillars and the panoramic windows. As jazzy Christmas music played through the speakers, Holly admired the restaurant's ambiance, with its elegant tables set with white linen tablecloths and red cloth napkins. The candles in the centerpieces were lit, giving the place an intimate feel.

The greeter offered them menus, and as Holly perused the names of the delectable dishes, she felt bubbly inside. Even if they didn't go dancing, this was enough for her: spending a lovely evening with close friends and family and enjoying a delicious meal.

After they placed their orders, Kim leaned forward. "All right, it wouldn't be a bachelorette party if we didn't talk about boys. So first: Nick. We can all agree that he's hot, right? I mean, well done, Holly. Seriously."

Holly giggled.

"That's a weird question for me to answer," Rachel said. "So I won't."

Lucy and Kim laughed.

"Fine, fine." Kim waved a dismissive hand at her. "Then I'll just say it. Nick is so hot."

Lucy put a hand on Rachel's arm. "Don't worry. Eddie's hot, too."

"And Sean," Kim added. "I mean, what's in the water in Silverwood that makes all the men here sexy?"

Vivian chuckled and then shushed the group. "They're going to kick us out before I can eat my duck."

The waiter brought the champagne Kim had ordered and poured

a serving for everyone.

"Ladies, raise your glasses," Kim announced. "And let's toast our Holly, who is arguably even hotter than Nick. May your marriage be blessed and last forever."

"Hear, hear!" Vivian said before sipping her champagne.

Kim, Lucy, and Holly all took a drink, but Rachel set down her glass.

"I thought you liked champagne," Holly said. "I've seen you drink it before."

Rachel shifted. "Yeah, no, I like it. I'm just, uh, waiting?"

"Waiting for what?" Lucy asked.

"Um …" Rachel rubbed her neck, looking around at the rest of them and shrugging.

"But it was a toast," Kim said. "You have to drink to the toast."

Holly narrowed her eyes. *Rachel didn't drink in the limo, either. Or at her house the other night.*

"Oh." Holly covered her mouth with her hand but quickly dropped it and cleared her throat. "Sorry. I shouldn't have, uh … No, it's fine. You don't have to, you know. Um, hey, should we talk about our hot men some more?"

Rachel's cheeks turned crimson.

"Oh em gee," Kim whispered. "Are you PG?"

Lucy and Vivian gaped at Rachel.

Holly playfully smacked Kim on the arm. "Kim, I was trying to *defuse* the bomb I just lit."

"It's okay," Rachel said with a laugh. "I guess the cat's already out of the bag. And we all know it's impossible to stuff that darned cat back in the bag." She paused for a second. "So, yes. Eddie and I are having another baby."

The table was filled with gasps, squeeing, and words of congratulations. Holly got goosebumps all over.

"Thank you." Rachel waved them off. "But no, stop. We wanted to wait until after Nick and Holly's wedding to say anything."

"But why?" Holly asked.

"We didn't want to steal any of the attention."

"Aw, Rachel, I wouldn't have thought you were trying to steal attention. I'm so happy for you. Now, I'm going to be the aunt to two little ones. That's amazing. Really, congratulations."

"Thank you. But for now, let's just keep it between us—and anyone within earshot of our table, I guess—until the wedding. We haven't told anyone yet. Not even Avery."

"Fine," Holly agreed.

"I'll drink to that," Kim joked, lifting her glass. "Our lips are sealed."

Two hours later, their spirits were high, and their bellies were full. Kim announced there was a VIP room in a club in the nearest city waiting for them. Holly would have normally called it a night, but exhilaration kept her going.

The night air was chilly and crisp compared to the warm restaurant. Kim sang a song while they made their way to the limousine, and Lucy tried to pull off a dance move that probably would have been executed better with less champagne in her system.

A shadowy figure watching them in the parking lot caught Holly's interest. She gasped and froze in place, her hand flying to her chest.

"Grayson?"

"Hello, Holly."

Dressed in all black, Grayson stood with his hands in his coat pockets. His lips were curled into a smug smile, his chin tilted upward. His dark-blond hair was slicked back, and his dark eyes were piercing.

A shiver ran down Holly's spine. *Am I imagining things? Is he really here?*

Judging by everyone else's expression, Grayson was no illusion.

"Wh-what are you doing here?" She didn't want Kim to be right. He couldn't possibly be in Silverwood to ruin her wedding, could he?

Kim set her jaw, her hands forming fists.

Holly held a hand up. "No, it's okay. Let me handle this." She swiveled and took three steps toward him. "What's the meaning of this, Grayson?"

Grayson smirked. "Don't you know, sweetheart? Doesn't the fact that I'm here show you how much I care for you?"

Holly ground her teeth. "You don't care about anyone but yourself."

"How can you say that? Don't you know I'm risking my job by being here instead? Don't you see the trouble you cause?"

"That's on you. Not me."

Grayson reached for her, and she pulled away.

"Aw, come on, baby." He flashed his devilish smile. "Don't be that way."

"What way would that be? Sensible? Full of self-respect? Smart enough not to fall for your tricks?"

"Difficult." He scoffed. "I mean, I went through the trouble of tracking you down to this middle of nowhere, Podunk little town, and you don't have the decency to have a civilized conversation with me."

"Do you hear yourself? How is stalking me civilized? We're not together and haven't been for over a year. There was no reason to track me down."

"Of course there was." Grayson jutted out a finger at her, his nostrils flaring. "I had to stop you from making the biggest mistake of your life. Well, the second-biggest mistake."

Holly shook her head. "How did you even find me?"

Grayson's gaze went momentarily to Kim. "Maybe some people

should pick better passwords, especially when they leave their offices unlocked."

Kim's jaw dropped before she muttered a curse.

Holly rolled her eyes and turned away from him. "This is ridiculous. You're beyond deranged, and I'm not even listening to you anymore."

"Oh, really, Holly? You don't think I can hold your attention?" His voice got louder the farther away she walked. "Did the caterer getting fired get your attention? Or the dress shop fire?"

She gasped and pivoted on her heel. "What?"

"How does he know about those things?" Rachel grumbled.

Kim marched forward. "*You* did those things?"

There was a glint of wickedness in Grayson's eyes. He shrugged and stuck his fists in his pockets. "Who knows? Bottom line is you don't know what I'm capable of."

"I should call the police," Holly said, her voice shaking.

"And say what? You can't prove anything."

"You just admitted—"

"I've admitted nothing. Maybe I'm just very observant."

Kim pointed a long, manicured nail at him. "You listen to me, you crazy stalker. If you so much as look Holly's way, I will be all over you like trolls on social media. Leave her alone, and don't even think about coming anywhere near the wedding. Like it or not, Holly is happy. She's getting married, come hell or high water, and there's nothing you can do to stop her."

Grayson scrubbed a hand over his jaw, backing away. "No one is afraid of you, Kim. Now who's being delusional?"

Vivian came to Kim's side, her nostrils flaring. "*Tumahimik ka!* Listen to me, you narcissistic devil animal. If you know what's good for you, you'll leave my daughter alone. You only think about yourself. Go back to whatever hole you climbed out of. No one wants you here. And just so you know, I never liked you. *Isa kang inutil!*"

Grayson's forehead wrinkled for a split second.

"You're *that* guy, aren't you?" Lucy said, coming forward next to Kim. "The one itching to have his butt kicked?"

His gaze went to Holly as he ground his teeth. "This isn't finished. Wait and see."

As he sauntered away, Holly felt like she was about to collapse. Her mother was quickly beside her, holding her steady and spouting off more harsh Tagalog phrases. Holly could feel tears forming, but she fought them off. She didn't want to give Grayson the pleasure of making her cry.

"He can't do anything," Rachel said, rubbing Holly's back. "I know the sheriff, and I'll ask him to have his team keep an eye out."

"I can't believe he was behind it all." Holly shook her head. "I have never hated anyone so much."

"You and me both," Rachel said.

Kim placed her palm on Holly's cheek. "Hey, you've got us. We won't allow anything bad to happen to this wedding."

"She's right," Lucy said. "He doesn't know what he's up against. Silverwood is a force to be reckoned with, and we take care of our own."

Holly sniffled, nodding. "Thank you, guys."

"Of course, honey." Kim hugged her.

It transformed into a group hug, and Holly felt a small sense of relief envelop her.

"Okay, let's not let Stalker Boy put a damper on this party." Kim clapped and raised her brows, her lips curling into a smile. "It's time to go dancing."

"Wait." Vivian wrung her hands together. "Are you sure that's a good idea? Maybe we need to be careful. Maybe we should take you home, Holly."

"No, it's fine." Holly raked her hair away from her face. "I won't permit Grayson to ruin anything. Not my bachelorette party, not my wedding, nothing. I won't give him that power."

"Sounds like the party's back on," Kim shouted.

Holly's friends *whooped* and hollered as they continued to the limo. Holly forced a smile, telling herself not to let Grayson spoil her night. She just hoped there was no muscle behind his threats.

Chapter Twenty-Three

T he windshield wipers pushed aside the fallen flakes as Nick
continued down the road. Holly sat in the passenger seat,
tapping her fingers in her lap, trying to figure out what he had
planned. They'd been on the road for a good hour, leaving Silverwood
far behind them.

"Where are we going?" Holly scanned their surroundings.

Nick gave her a sideways grin. "I already told you. It's a surprise."

"Nick, I have a confession to make." Holly settled a hand on his
arm. "I hate surprises."

"Well, then, I guess it's my mission to change your mind."

"Wait." Holly narrowed her eyes. "Has this all been a ruse? A
year-long, elaborate scheme to gain my trust so that you could kidnap
me?"

"Oh no," Nick deadpanned. "You've cracked my devious plan to
trap you in Silverwood forever."

"Well, the joke's on you because I happen to love it here."

Holly watched the snow fall, counting in her head to keep from
begging Nick to tell her what he was up to. Just as she was about to
nag him again, a sign on the road ahead caught her eye.

"The Christmas tree maze?" Holly inched forward. "Is that where
we're going?"

There was a twinkle in Nick's eyes.

A bubbling excitement rose in Holly's stomach. She remembered
seeing an ad about a wintery maze made of decorated Christmas trees,

but with all the wedding planning, she hadn't given it much thought. However, after the confrontation with Grayson the night before, Holly figured she could use a fun, worry-free evening.

They pulled into the parking lot of the maze event as the sun kissed the peaks of the mountains in the distance. Nick let Cupid out of the back of the SUV before going to Holly's side. He held her hand as they walked to the ticket booth. Children ran past them, laughing and shouting in glee, eager to partake in the game.

The stars above mirrored the twinkling lights of the Christmas trees in the large plot of land before them. The maze owners had to be counting themselves lucky that the recent storm hadn't reached their area. The air was crisp, but the wind gentle, allowing the flurries to fall softly to the ground.

Holly's boots crunched in the snow as they approached the booth.

"Two, please," Nick said to the woman behind the counter.

"The maze is free." The older woman, whose name tag read Heather, had a thick southern accent. "We do take donations, of course, which we forward to a few charities."

"That sounds perfect." Nick handed her some cash. "There you go."

"Thank you so much." Heather exchanged Nick's money for two small green tickets. "Have you ever done the maze before?"

"I've done a corn maze," Nick replied. "Holly?"

"No. This will be my first time."

"Well, okay." Heather leaned on her elbows. "It works just like a corn maze or a haybale maze. You'll be starting at the entrance right behind me, and you'll make your way through, searching for the exit. We've got attendants with lit-up reindeer antlers and reflective vests inside, so if you get lost, don't worry. We encourage you to enjoy yourself, but please refrain from removing or damaging any tree ornaments. Remember, Santa is watching." Heather playfully tapped a finger on the side of her nose.

Nick nodded. "Understood."

Heather smiled at them. "Can I just say something? You make a very handsome couple."

"Thank you, Heather. That's awfully nice of you to say." Nick put an arm around Holly. "We're, uh, getting married in a couple days. On New Year's Eve day, to be exact."

"Aw, married. How wonderful. Congratulations."

"Thank you," Holly and Nick said together.

Heather straightened. "You must be excited."

"Yeah." Holly interlaced her fingers. "A little nervous. Not about *being* married, but about the actual day."

"Aw, honey, let me tell you." Heather chuckled and shook her head. "My wedding took place during a hurricane. My Don and I lived down south, and despite planning out our wedding to the most minor detail, we just couldn't account for a storm hitting us. It was the worst uninvited guest anyone could ask for."

"Oh no." Holly's heart broke for the woman.

"Talk about inconvenient," Nick said.

Heather chuckled again. "It was. Our venue was flooded, and the hurricane stranded half the guests."

Holly shook her head. "I think I would have lost my mind."

"Honey, I nearly did. But in the end, all of that didn't matter. Don and I got hitched at the local fire station, and we laugh about our little adventure now. It makes for a fun story, at the very least. And we've been married for nearly forty years now."

"That's great, Heather," Nick said. "Congratulations."

"Appreciate it. And good luck to you both."

"Thanks. So, is the maze tricky?" Holly asked.

Heather leaned forward once more. "Like most things in life, it wouldn't be worth the trouble if it were easy."

"Well, we might have an advantage." Nick gestured at Cupid, who was sitting on his haunches, waiting. "We've got a pretty intuitive snow dog to help us out."

"That is, unless a squirrel crosses his path," Holly added.

Heather snorted. "Well, let's hope that doesn't happen. Gorgeous dog, though. Husky?"

"Malamute," Nick responded.

"He's a beaut. In any case, you'll want to get to the end of the maze, for sure." Heather looked left and right as if she was about to let them in on a secret and didn't want anyone else to hear. "When you get to the exit, there's a special wish box. You write down your New Year's wish on a card available there, drop it in the box, and your wish just might come true in the coming year."

"How fun." Holly stuffed her hands in her coat pockets. "We'll definitely make some New Year's wishes."

Nick glanced at Holly. "Not sure what I should write down. My wish already came true."

Holly's cheeks grew warmer. She turned from him to Heather. "Thanks again."

"Enjoy the maze," Heather replied with a wave.

With a nod, Nick hung his arm over Holly's shoulders. They made their way past the booth and through the entrance, marked with a big, red arrow.

The sky darkened as Nick and Holly entered the maze. What seemed like a hundred Christmas trees encircled them, twinkling lights glowing everywhere. The snow came down in gentle waves, flakes landing on her nose and cheeks as Nick and Holly walked languidly through a literal winter wonderland.

Nick tucked the ticket stubs into his pocket before taking Holly's hand.

Cupid trotted in front of them, sniffing the snow and the lower branches of the trees. It was quiet, with no music playing. The only sound that interrupted the silence was the bubble of children's laughter. A peaceful calm surrounded Holly, easing her tension.

"This is beautiful." Holly squeezed Nick's hand. "One might say, 'a-*maze*-ing.'"

Nick sucked in a breath through his teeth. "Yikes. It's a good thing you're cute."

Holly playfully elbowed him. "But honestly, it's mesmerizing. I almost don't want to find my way out."

"We could make it work," Nick joked. "I'm pretty handy with tools. I could build us a little hut. The place has lighting, so that wouldn't be an issue, and we have each other to keep warm."

"There is a ton of foot traffic, though. So, not a lot of privacy." Holly scrunched her nose.

They reached an intersection where they had to choose whether to go left or right.

"Which way?" Holly asked.

Cupid sniffed the air in front of them and then scurried to the right.

Nick smiled. "I say we trust the snow scout."

Nick and Holly continued on their way, allowing Cupid to lead them through the trees. Holly leaned her head back to take in the panoramic view of the stars. She felt like she was in another world, one with no worries. Snowflakes landed on her face, but she welcomed them.

Nick's arm came around her waist, and she realized they were making yet another turn.

"So, listen," Nick began.

Holly stopped abruptly. "Oh, no."

A crease formed between Nick's brows. "What?"

WEDDING BELLS IN SILVERWOOD

"You're getting cold feet, aren't you?"

Nick let out a small laugh. "What? No."

"You are." Holly shivered. "You've got cold feet, you can't stand my corny jokes, so you're breaking up with me and abandoning me in this labyrinth, and you're about to run off through the trees in hopes I can't find my way out."

Nick pulled her into his arms. "You've got quite the imagination, you know that?"

Holly chewed her lip and averted her gaze. "Or maybe I've been struck down one too many times and can't get out of the habit of waiting for the other shoe to drop."

Nick lifted her chin and gazed into her eyes. "There will be no shoe dropping on my watch."

She bit the inside of her cheek. His expression told her he had something on his mind.

"What, then?" she asked. "What is it?"

"Were you not listening when I said you can talk to me when something burdens you?"

She tensed. "I was."

"So why didn't you tell me Grayson showed up in Silverwood and threatened you?"

She felt as if she couldn't catch her breath. "I … I don't know. I think I just wanted to block out the whole incident from my mind."

"I'd like to think we have a healthy relationship."

"We do," she proclaimed earnestly.

"Then we always have to be honest with each other. That includes letting one another know the important things. No omissions of truth."

She dropped her gaze. "You're right. I'm sorry."

"Holly, Grayson sounds delusional and dangerous. It kills me that I wasn't there to give him a stern talking-to, and it kills me even more that he tormented you. I've got to tell you, I'm a peaceful man, but when Rachel told me how he showed up terrorizing you? That might have been the first time I've wanted to kick someone's teeth in."

Holly grasped Nick's coat. "I just … I can't fathom that he's in Silverwood. I want to believe that his bark is worse than his bite, but at the same time, I'm terrified he's going to do something stupid to ruin the wedding."

Nick sighed and held her tightly. "The police have been alerted. Everyone is on the lookout. I'll do everything in my power to stop him from ruining anything. I've sort of got connections, you know?"

Despite her anxiety, Holly smiled.

"And in the end, he loses anyway." Nick leaned back to look at her. "Because *I'm* the one marrying you, not him. And there's no way he's going to change that."

"You seem so calm," Holly said. "Am I crazy for freaking out?"

"No. You're just cautious. But don't worry. Everything's going to be fine. Look at Heather and her hurricane wedding. Even if all our plans fall apart, we've already come out ahead as long as we have each other. There's a reason why they're called 'silver linings.' Hidden by those clouds, there's still a sun shining behind it all."

She winced. "That might be a little cheesy, even for me."

He let out a low chuckle. "Well, sometimes I'm a little cheesy."

She lifted a brow, her arms tightening around him. "So, no cold feet?"

"The exact opposite. I've got hot feet."

Holly laughed. "What?"

"I can't wait to marry you."

Giggling, Holly stood on her tiptoes and placed a kiss on Nick's lips. "So you *do* like my corny jokes?"

"Well, let's not get carried away."

Chapter Twenty-Four

T oday is a new day.

Holly stared into the mirror, her fingers running along the smooth material of the wedding dress her mother had brought from the Philippines. It really was stunning, and Holly felt proud to represent her heritage on this special occasion.

She turned her head to inspect her hair. It was swept up into an elegant twist that flattered her neck. Every strand was perfectly in place. Her veil—which she had luckily taken home before the boutique fire—was pinned to the back of her head, flowing down to the middle of her back. The Mason family brooch was on display on the front of her dress.

Her makeup was impeccable, and her white, satin shoes didn't pinch her feet.

So far, so good.

Holding a hand to her stomach to still the jitters, she stepped out of the changing room and into the hall.

Her guests' voices drifted up to her from the chateau's entrance. Friends and family greeted each other, commented on how lovely the venue was, and exchanged small talk.

Holly kept out of sight in the upstairs hall. She paced back from the banister, taking slow breaths and ignoring the heavy beat of her heart.

Today is a good day.

Whispers found her ears. Spotting Rachel and Lucy at the end of the hall, Holly held her breath. Their set jaws and lowered brows triggered alarms in her head. The whispers were theirs, but when they noticed Holly, they stopped talking and straightened.

No, no, no. Today's supposed to be a good day.

Holly walked toward them, the hold on her stomach tightening. "What? What is it?"

Several scenarios zipped through her mind. At the top of the list was the possibility that Nick had decided not to marry her.

"Oh, Holly." Lucy smiled, all traces of apprehension gone. "You look beautiful."

"Lucy, thank you, but please tell me what's going on."

Lucy looked at Rachel, seemingly lost for what to say.

Rachel gently took hold of Holly's arm. "Don't freak out, okay? Sheriff Barnes called to inform us that Grayson's been spotted around Silverwood. Some citizens phoned in to report sightings, but Barnes's officers couldn't find him."

"He's eluding them," Lucy added. "But they've got roadblocks set up on all the roads leading here, so I doubt he'll get through."

Holly didn't agree. She knew Grayson would stop at nothing to see his plan through. But she didn't want to get worked up. *Think positive.* "Okay. Okay."

Lucy and Rachel exchanged a look.

Holly's shoulders slumped. "There's more?"

"Just a few delays." Rachel shook her head. "Nothing you should stress about."

"Delays?" Holly wrung her hands. "Tell me."

"The florist called because someone tried to cancel the flower delivery." Lucy put her hand up, palms facing Holly. "But it's a good thing we know the florist, who also happens to be a guest. Melissa knew the wedding hadn't been canceled. She alerted the shop and *un*canceled the order. They should be delivering any minute now."

"But the guests have already started to arrive." Holly bit her lip.

"Don't worry," Rachel said. "We've kept them in the main room and won't allow them in the winter garden until the flowers are set up. Kim is keeping them entertained. And I think she's enjoying the limelight."

"We have to wait for Father William anyway." Lucy cringed as soon as she said it.

Holly's eyes widened. "Wait for him? What do you mean?"

"He got stuck at his apartment. Apparently, he has two flat tires."

"But we've got it under control," Rachel said. "Eddie called one of his buddies to drive out and give him a ride."

"They'll be here soon," Lucy added.

Holly rubbed her neck, which felt unbearably hot. "This is all Grayson's doing. I can't believe this. I wish I'd never met the creep."

"Holly, breathe." Rachel held Holly's shoulders. "We've got it under control. He's not going to ruin the wedding."

Nausea reared its ugly head. Holly covered her mouth and ran toward the changing room, slamming the door behind her. *Oh, God. He's doing it, isn't he? Grayson's ruining my wedding.* Pressing her back against the door, she fought to catch her breath and not empty her stomach.

She couldn't get any air. The walls were closing in. There were two windows in the room. Despite the chilly weather, Holly hurried and opened each, but it was still too hot. Holly wasn't sure what hyperventilating felt like, but this had to be it. She paced the small room, pushing down on her abdomen to get the churning to stop, all while sucking in deep gulps of oxygen.

Is there even air in this room? It didn't feel like it.

A knock at the door made her jump. With everything going wrong, she was glad her gasp hadn't caused the bodice of her dress to rip.

"Holly, are you okay?" Her mother cracked open the door and peeked inside. "Rachel and Lucy said you went pale. Kim thinks you're climbing out the window and running back to New York." Vivian glanced at the open windows. "Maybe she's more intuitive than I thought."

Holly's knees felt weak. She wasn't convinced her legs would hold her up anymore. She settled in a chair, forcing herself to take deep breaths.

Vivian stepped into the room and shut the door. She wrapped her arms around herself. "It's freezing in here. Is it okay if I close the windows?"

Holly nodded, biting her lip.

Vivian's dress swished as she moved. "That's better." She sat next to Holly and ran a hand down her arm. "Now we just have to get the chill out of you."

Holly blew out a shuddered breath. It was only a matter of seconds before the threat of tears spilling over onto her cheeks would become a reality. "Mom, do you believe in signs?"

Vivian took Holly's hands in hers. "Holly, these are just hiccups. Maybe even little tests. Things go wrong. You can't control everything. But you can choose what to do with the hand you're dealt."

"This is supposed to be the happiest day of my life. I didn't want to believe Grayson could ruin it, but look at all the chaos he's created."

"Think of it as failed attempts," Vivian said. "Whatever he threw your way was overcome. We matched him, play by play, move for move. Don't focus on what's going wrong. There's always a way to turn it around."

"You don't think this is the universe's way of telling me I

shouldn't be getting married? I mean, Nick and I have only been together for a year. Maybe we rushed into this."

"No. Not at all." Vivian trailed her fingers along Holly's veil. "If I were certain of anything at all, it's that you and Nick belong together. I've seen how he looks at you and you at him. I can practically feel the chemistry. It checks all the boxes."

Holly mustered up a small smile. "Really?"

"Definitely. Couple goals, as they say." Vivian chuckled. "You know how long my parents—your *lolo* and *lola*—knew each other before they got engaged?"

"No."

"About six weeks. And they got married two months later."

"Wow. Okay, that's fast."

"And they're still together. Because they knew it was right."

Holly grinned.

"As for all the little glitches," Vivian said, half-shrugging, "I heard an adage once that stayed with me. *You can't stop the waves, but you can learn to swim.*"

Holly scoffed. "Maybe I've exaggerated it all in my mind, but I feel like I'm barely keeping afloat."

"Honey. You're sailing." Vivian adjusted Holly's veil. "So, no. I don't think there are any signs saying you shouldn't get married. I think the signs are saying you and Nick are strong."

A knock at the door interrupted them.

Vivian patted her daughter's hand and stood. "Who is it?"

"It's me," Nick answered.

Holly jumped to her feet and hurried to the door. "You can't come in."

"I know," he said. "I'm not going to tempt fate. Don't worry. I just wanted to check on you."

Holly and Vivian exchanged a look.

"We can crack the door open," Vivian suggested. "Only enough so you can hear each other. But no peeking."

Nick laughed. "No peeking, I promise."

Vivian turned the knob and opened the door an inch. Then she backed away, sitting on the chair at the far end of the room to give them space.

"So I take it you heard," Nick said.

Holly held her hands to her chest. "I did. And I'm sorry. I told you I have baggage. This is what happens when you have baggage."

"This isn't your fault, Holly. You are the victim here. And everything's been dealt with. We're battling off the hurricane."

Vivian wrinkled her brow. Holly waved a hand at her.

"He's trying to intimidate us. That's all," Nick said. "Don't let him. You know the saying, 'No one can make you feel inferior without your consent.'"

"Sounds like something your dad would say."

"Actually, it's Eleanor Roosevelt."

Holly sighed. "I don't want him to ruin our day."

"Say the word, and we'll run away now. Elope."

"You'd do that?"

"For you? Yes. In a heartbeat. I would marry you in a monsoon. I would marry you in a landfill. All that matters is that I get to spend every day with the love of my life from here on out."

Holly traced the carvings in the door with her finger. "That's all I want, too."

"Holly, I can't wait to marry you. I can't wait to share a thousand adventures with you. Because no matter what life throws at us, I know that with you, it will be incredible."

The churning in her stomach disappeared, replaced by hope. "Then I guess we should get married."

Nick chuckled. "Sounds like a plan. Rachel will tell you when everything's ready to go."

"Nick?"

"Yeah?"

She rested her head against the door. "I love you."

"I love you, too."

Chapter Twenty-Five

Viola circled the kitchen once more. She'd already triple-checked that every station was prepared and nothing was missing. Her crew was all present and accounted for, each in their proper attire, cutting and slicing the garnish for the meals Viola had spent hours cooking. The dishes sat warm in their insolated containers, and the appetizers were ready for the reception.

Though she had a timeline planned out, it had to be adjusted. Christelle, who was helping in the kitchen, had found out that the ceremony hadn't begun yet and told Viola. Apparently, a few things were causing delays. She pushed down her anxiety and told herself everything would be fine.

Viola blew out a controlled breath as she stepped through the double doors into the dining room. Oliver was busy with the final touches, ensuring every piece of silverware was lined up and the napkins were all folded properly.

"Looks great, Oliver." Viola walked over to him and smoothed out the tablecloth.

"Good thing I have years of experience setting formal tableware."

"Holly and Nick are going to love it."

Oliver raised his brows. "I'd like to think they'll be too preoccupied gazing into each other's eyes to even notice the fancy dishes."

"As much as I'm a fan of love," Viola began, "I do hope my culinary skills are impressive enough for them to notice so I can get more of these gigs."

"Oh, I'm positive they will." Oliver stuck a hand in his pocket. "Speaking of love."

Viola narrowed her eyes, wondering what he was up to. Oliver opened a little black box to reveal a slim silver ring with a teardrop-shaped diamond. Viola gasped.

"I'm going to ask Amy to marry me." Oliver's smile was so big it nearly split his face.

Viola did a little jump, her hands flying to her cheeks. She was barely aware of a door swinging open somewhere as she rose on her tiptoes to embrace her friend.

"That's amazing. I'm so happy for you."

"Thank you." Oliver patted her on the back before releasing her. "But she hasn't said yes yet."

"I have a feeling she will."

His cheeks reddened. "You don't think it's too cliché? Getting engaged on New Year's Eve?"

"Not at all. And hey, if you need a caterer for your wedding …"

Oliver laughed and tucked the ring box back in his pocket. "You're at the top of my list."

Viola glanced around. The door to the dining room swung slightly as if someone had entered, but she didn't see anyone. Had a guest or wedding party member opened the door and then decided not to come in? When the timer on Viola's watch beeped, she dismissed the thought and smiled at her friend.

"I'm going to see where we stand, timewise. We were supposed to be serving the appetizers by now."

Viola straightened her chef's jacket and hiked through the chateau toward the winter garden. Delays in ceremonies were common, but in order to get the timing right for serving the food, she needed to check what was happening with the bride and groom.

When she reached the winter garden, Viola became mesmerized. The afternoon sun could be seen through the wedding arch and the glass doors beyond it. The elegant white chairs were lined up in perfect rows. At equidistant intervals stood large ivory stone vases filled with pink roses, lilacs, freesia, and sprigs of baby's breath.

The guests were seated, waiting for the ceremony to begin. She wasn't certain whom to ask for an update but figured the wedding would still be taking place since the invitees were still there. As Viola was about to head back to the kitchen, she spotted Jonas standing at the back of the room. His dark gray suit was tailored perfectly to fit his form. He was clean-shaven, and not a hair on his head was out of place. Their eyes locked for a moment, and the green of his sparkled. Viola smiled at him, but he averted his gaze.

Someone's in a bad mood today.

Viola reminded herself how serious Jonas was about work. He wasn't a guest at the wedding; this was all business for him.

She put on a pleasant expression and approached him. "You look nice," she whispered.

His smile appeared forced. Viola chalked it up to him focusing on being professional and not allowing himself to loosen up.

"Any idea what the holdup is?" she asked, sensing the need to shift the conversation.

"Probably cold feet." Jonas adjusted his tie, not looking at her. "Sometimes people don't realize until the last second that the decisions they made were the wrong ones."

"What? No, I don't think that's what's happening. Holly and Nick? That's a sure thing. Guaranteed."

"I don't believe sure things exist."

Jonas turned to her. She couldn't read his expression, but the icy look in his eyes sent a rush of acid to her stomach.

"I thought you should know," he began, "I'm leaving

Silverwood."

Viola blinked. "You … What?"

"Some things have, uh, changed my perspective, and I've decided to concentrate on my business in Billings. So I'm selling the chateau."

"But …" Her chest hitched. She took a breath, but her lungs constricted. She felt a pain that made her think her heart had stopped. *What changed? Did I do something? Or has he realized he only cares about where the money is?* Viola wrung her hands. "When are you leaving?"

He looked away from her, straightening his cufflinks. "As soon as I can get all my affairs in order."

"I see."

Her throat went dry, making it hard to swallow.

The harmonic sound of the string quartet filled the room, and a chill ran down Viola's spine.

Her head spun. She was only remotely aware that the priest and Nick had passed her to take their positions at the altar. A mumbling of low voices broke the silence, and she realized the groomsmen and bridesmaids had gathered at the back of the room.

From the corner of her eye, she caught a glimpse of white. She swiveled her head to see the beautiful bride. *Looks like we're back on track.* Viola opened her mouth, about to tell Jonas she was heading back to the kitchen, but she couldn't get her voice to work.

As the music swelled for Holly's walk down the aisle, Viola felt like her heart was being crushed.

Chapter Twenty-Six

Holly's hands were trembling so much she thought she might drop her bouquet. The only thing preventing her from collapsing was her mother's sturdy arm. With music filling the room, Holly took controlled breaths as the groomsmen and bridesmaids began their procession down the aisle, two by two.

It's happening. It's happening.

Holly's head swirled. She felt it was a dream and had to blink multiple times to take it all in.

Their priest, Father William, stood at the altar. The first to reach him were Lucy and Sean. They unhooked their arms at the arch and went left and right, respectively. After them came Kim and Eddie. Then, the Matron of Honor and Best Man, Rachel, and Mr. Mason.

Once everyone had taken their positions, Cupid and Avery walked side-by-side. A leather pouch containing Nick and Holly's rings was attached to Cupid's collar. Cupid trotted forward as Avery spread light pink flower petals along the ivory runner. Cupid's eight siblings, all positioned near the aisle, panted as they watched their prominent brother strut past them.

When Cupid and Avery arrived at the arch, the music changed. The guests all faced Holly as Mendelssohn's "Wedding March" began. As everyone stood, Holly felt her heart freefall into her stomach. It took all her strength not to collapse on the spot.

"Are you all right, sweetheart?" Vivian whispered.

"I don't know if I can move my legs." Holly spoke so quietly that she wasn't sure her mother heard her.

Vivian gave her a nod. "I'm right here. You can do this."

"I wish Dad were here, too."

Vivian smiled at her. "He's here, honey. I feel it. And I know he's very, very proud of the woman you turned out to be."

Holly nearly lost it, but she sucked back the tears and straightened her shoulders. "It feels like that arch is miles away."

"Holly, even the mightiest of mountains is conquered one step at a time."

Holly swallowed hard, attempting to unclench all her muscles. The music continued, but her feet wouldn't budge.

And then Nick, who stood facing the priest at the altar, turned around. When his eyes met hers, Holly's lungs filled with the sweetest, warmest air. The light-hearted feeling spread throughout her body until she felt as if she were floating.

She took a step and advanced to the beat of the music. Her heart wanted to be closer to Nick, so she followed her heart.

Though she felt the eyes of their guests on her, her focus remained on Nick, whose soft smile caused a warm glow to swell in her chest.

Holly and Vivian stopped at the arch. The heady scent of freesia and lilacs wafted around her. With a sigh, Vivian leaned close to Holly and placed a gentle palm on her cheek.

"I love you, sweetheart." Vivian's voice broke on the last word.

"I love you too, Mom." Holly waged an inner battle to hold back the surge of sentimental tears.

Vivian wasn't as successful as Holly in keeping her tears at bay as she kissed Holly's cheek. Holly let out a shuddering breath as her mother released her and went to take her seat.

Swallowing the lump in her throat, Holly swiveled to face Nick. She stepped under the wedding arch and gazed into his eyes.

This feels so right. I'm not afraid anymore.

Father William instructed the invitees to sit. As he continued welcoming everyone in the name of celebrating Nick and Holly's love, Holly became strongly aware of her heartbeat. She listened to the priest's words, feeling their importance, but she couldn't tear her eyes off Nick. Handsome didn't begin to cover it. He was dashing. Dare she say debonaire? Perhaps there wasn't a proper word to describe how he looked. He was everything, all she ever wanted and all she would ever need.

Holly was highly conscious that everyone was watching her and that she and Nick were the center of attention. Though part of her mind was focused on the logistics of the ceremony, the emotional part of her brain was swooning. She was almost lost in disbelief that she and Nick were finally becoming one, knowing that in a matter of minutes, they would be bound to each other forever, that this was the beginning of her brand-new life. Her body tingled all over, and the giddiness made her grin.

"Dear friends," Father William said, "Nick and Holly have prepared their vows, and it is their wish to recite them now in the presence of their family and loved ones."

Father William folded his hands and gave Nick a nod.

Nick returned the nod and took a deep breath. "Holly. From the first moment I saw you, I was under your spell. And I will willingly remain under this sweet, euphoric, intoxicating spell you've cast until time ends and the stars fade to black. Because with you, I feel young again. I feel whole. Complete. This"—he gestured between them— "makes sense. Every day, you take my breath away. I keep thinking this could all be a dream. If it is, I never want to wake up. I count myself lucky to stand beside you. Not just now, but through the years, for better or worse, and in every moment, every breath, my love for you will be there."

Holly could have swooned. She took a second, letting Nick's words seep into her heart and soul.

Father William looked her way, and she prepared herself for her turn.

"Nick." Holly swallowed back happy tears. "Nicky. You're such a good person. Such a good man. I can't believe how blessed I am to have you in my world. To have you in my heart. As long as you are with me, I'm home. I was lost, and then I found you. You make me feel like I am exactly where I belong. And I want that feeling for the rest of my life. These last few weeks have shown me that we can't predict what the future brings and what obstacles will be thrown in our way. But I know that as long as you're with me and I have your love, you will have mine, and we can make it through anything."

Father William raised his hands out at his sides. "May we please have the rings?"

Nick clicked his tongue, and Cupid came over to stand between him and Holly. Avery followed, crouching to retrieve the bands from the pouch Cupid wore. With a huge smile, Avery handed the corresponding rings to Nick and Holly. Holly passed her bouquet to Rachel.

"Holly and Nick, as you prepare to follow the path of marriage, I now ask for you to state your intentions. Do you, Nicholas Mason Jr., take Holly St. Ives to be your wife? Do you promise to be faithful to her, in good times and in bad, in sickness and health, to love and honor her all the days of your life?"

Though his eyes glistened with tears, Nick smiled. "I do." He slipped the ring on her finger and squeezed her hand.

"Do you, Holly," Father William continued, "take Nicholas Mason Jr. to be your husband? Do you promise to be faithful to him, in good times and in bad, in sickness and health, to love and honor him all the days of your life?"

"I do." Holly wasn't sure anyone heard her over the pounding of her heart. She slipped the ring onto his finger and then held on to his hands.

Father William smiled. "In sight of God and these witnesses, I now pronounce you husband and wife. Nick, you may kiss your bride."

As Holly and Nick leaned in for their kiss, the guests rose to their feet and applauded. Wedding bells rang, echoing around them.

Father Williams raised his voice to be heard over the applause. "Ladies, gentlemen, and four-legged friends, for the first time ever, I introduce to you Mr. and Mrs. Nick and Holly Ma—"

"Holly, no!"

Gasps filled the winter garden as Grayson charged in, dragging Susan along with him despite her attempts to pull him back.

"Oh no." Holly tensed, her neck aching from the sudden movement. "Grayson."

Nick squared his shoulders. "How'd he—?"

"I'm sorry." Frazzled, Susan smoothed her hair into place. "I tried to stop him."

"Holly," Grayson interrupted. "We have unfinished business."

Sean, Eddie, and Rachel looked between themselves and Nick, unsure what to do. Nick shook his head, a silent plea in his eyes, urging them not to take any action. Holly was frozen, unable to move—unable to believe this was happening.

"Son," Father Williams said calmly. "You're too late."

"It's never too late," Grayson insisted. "Holly and I belong together."

"No, Grayson," Holly said, her voice weak. "I'm with Nick. We're married now."

"Do you have any idea what lengths I went to prove my love for you?" Grayson's hands were balled into fists.

The crowd murmured, clearly confused.

"Do you know how much I had to pay that caterer worker to look through the files for your address? Only for him to get fired and the company to lose their contract? He wouldn't give me the address after that, so I was out that cash."

Holly's jaw dropped in disbelief.

"Can you imagine how hard it was for me to stand in that storm?" Grayson continued. "How difficult it was for me to get that branch through the dress shop window? I did that for you, Holly. That's how much you mean to me."

Holly felt the tears forming in her eyes. "You're a sociopath."

"But do you appreciate my efforts? Do you not see how hard I'm fighting for you?"

"Young man," Father William said, his tone harsher now, "I suggest you leave the premises immediately."

Grayson ignored him. "You know we're meant to be, Holly," he went on. "I forgive you for not yet realizing it. What do you say? Bygones?"

Holly ground her teeth. "The only bygones happening here is me saying bye and you being gone."

"You heard her," Nick said, stepping closer to Grayson. "It's time for you to leave."

"Don't touch me." Grayson sneered as he backed up. He noticed that Eddie, Sean, and the priest were all reaching for him. In his attempt to avoid their reach, he twisted, his arms flailing. The back of his foot caught on the altar's base, and he lost his balance.

Grayson fell backward, barreling into the wedding arch. A crack resounded, followed by gasps from everyone in the room. The arch teetered, and Nick pulled Holly into his arms and out of harm's way as it collapsed. Grayson was on the floor among the splinters, looking up at them with wide eyes.

Cupid let out a deep growl. As the first bark exploded through the room, it triggered the response of his siblings. Dasher slunk forward first, teeth bared. Dancer, Prancer, Vixen, Comet, Donner, Blitzen, and Rudolph traveled as a pack, all growling and snarling.

Grayson visibly swallowed, sweat forming on his brow. He scrambled to his feet and turned on his heel, pushing Father William out of his way as he darted toward the glass double doors. Knocking down a standing vase full of flowers, he tore the doors open and charged outside.

Cupid and his siblings stampeded after him. Their barks echoed through the frosty air. Dasher's howl followed immediately after Cupid's, which set off the yelps of the other dogs. Nick, Holly, and their guests hurried after the hounds. Their shrieks and hollers were drowned out by the cacophony of all nine Alaskan Malamutes barking and howling as they chased after the wedding crasher.

Nick stuck his thumb and forefinger between his teeth and whistled, but the dogs couldn't be stopped. They were on an inexorable mission to chase down the threat.

The scarf that hung loosely from Grayson's neck flew off. Grayson kicked up waves of snow as he scurried from the scene, desperate to outrun his pursuers. Holly saw him twist his head left and right but continue forward.

Right toward the frozen lake.

Oh no. Holly remembered the "Thin Ice" sign, which had been blocking the lake for weeks now.

The dogs had Grayson cut off from the shore. He darted onto the ice seemingly without thinking.

"Grayson, stop!" Nick called.

Grayson didn't stop.

The entire wedding party and their guests gathered on the shore of the lake, incredulous as to what they were witnessing.

WEDDING BELLS IN SILVERWOOD

Cupid and his siblings slowed, not venturing any farther, but their howls and barks continued.

Before the sound of the crack reached her ears, one of Grayson's legs disappeared beneath the ice. Holly was sure Grayson shrieked, but it was lost in the assemblage of noise coming from their friends and family.

Nick moved onto the frozen lake, slipping along the surface but holding his balance. "Grayson, hold on!"

"Nick, don't!" Holly called after him. Her breathing was rushed, and her head swirled.

Grayson slipped some more, the lower half of his body below the lake's surface.

"I've got some rope," Jonas called out as he doubled back to the building.

Holly's pulse hammered. Grayson's eyes were wild with panic as he clung to the ice's edge. The dogs had stopped howling, instead resorting to pacing near Grayson. They were careful enough to keep a distance from the danger zone.

Holly felt someone grab her arm and turned to see her mother, who mumbled something in Tagalog.

Holly put her arm around her mom. "It's going to be okay."

It felt like forever before Jonas had returned with a long, thick rope. All the while, Nick inched forward, trying to find a spot close enough to Grayson without endangering himself.

Jonas ran out to Nick, handing him some of the rope, and the two of them drew closer to the thin ice. Holly fleetingly wondered what the rope's regular purpose was when it wasn't being pulled out for a rescue.

Nick yelled something at Jonas that Holly couldn't quite understand. Then, one end of the rope was hurled through the air toward Grayson, who struggled to catch it while clinging to the ice shelf for dear life.

Nick and Jonas wrapped their arms through the other end of the rope. They tried to pull but kept slipping along the icy surface, unable to get enough grip. A loud whistle hit the air, and the team of Malamutes promptly scooted forward. Each dog lined up and grabbed the rope with their mouths, and together with Nick's instructions, they yanked the half-submerged Grayson out of the lake. They didn't stop pulling until Grayson was clear, dragging him on his belly over the slippery surface.

Once Grayson was safe, Nick helped him up and supported his weight, assisting him back toward the building.

"Give them room," Father William shouted. "We should all go back inside."

The guests backed up but lingered, stunned by the incident and shivering from the chilly weather.

Grayson, being escorted by Nick, was soaked through and clearly frazzled. His eyes darted around the crowd of wedding guests. His fingers and ears were bright red, and his lips were turning blue.

"You're going to need to get out of those wet clothes and warm up," Nick told him. "You don't want hypothermia to set in. I think we might have something to change into inside."

"We've got some blankets," Jonas said. "I'll ask Susan to get them."

Grayson's brow furrowed as he stared at Nick. He looked defeated, standing there soaking wet and red in the face. "Wh-why are you helping me? I sabotaged your wedding. I've made the last few weeks a nightmare for you."

Nick sighed and patted him on the back. "It's the right thing to do. However awful you've been, you don't deserve to die. We can deal with the consequences later."

"I've already called the police," Jonas added.

"Then I guess we'll deal with the consequences sooner than we thought." Nick shrugged and placed an arm around Holly.

Grayson turned to face Holly. He shivered and sniffled, and the corners of his mouth drew downward. "Holly. I don't know what to say. I'm sorry."

Holly held on to Nick. She had a feeling Grayson was only sorry he'd been caught. Still, she didn't want him to have anything more to do with her special day. The police were on their way, and Grayson would be locked up for several charges.

"It stops now," she said. "It's over."

Grayson stared at her for what seemed like forever. And then he nodded, and Holly averted her gaze.

Eddie and Jonas had a grip on each of Grayson's arms. They escorted him somewhere to be detained until the cops showed up.

"Are you all right?" Holly asked Nick.

"I'm fine. Are you okay? You didn't get hurt, did you?"

"Not physically, no."

"The worst is over." Nick lifted Holly's chin with a finger. "I did promise you a life of adventure, didn't I?"

Holly couldn't help but laugh. "This isn't exactly what I had in mind."

Nick's smile grew wider. "Well, don't let the drama get you down. After all, we've got a party to throw, Mrs. Mason."

Holly leaned into him. "I do like the sound of that."

Chapter Twenty-Seven

Viola stood near the kitchen doors, watching the newlyweds dance to a slow love song. Holly and Nick oozed affection, and Nick looked at his bride with a tender gaze that seemed unbreakable.

Sighing, Viola assessed how the evening had gone. The guests devoured the appetizers until there was none left. Oliver and the other wait staff said the main courses had been a hit. Viola mentally patted herself on the back for getting all the meals served on time and ensuring the quality, temperature, and taste were up to her standards.

My cooking teacher would be proud.

She was especially pleased with how the cake turned out. Though she'd baked many a cake and torte, this was the first three-tier wedding cake she'd ever made. All in all, as Viola reflected on the evening as it was coming to an end, she considered her first catering job a success.

Jonas entered the dining hall, and Viola sucked in a breath. His eyes met hers for a moment before he adjusted his cufflinks and pivoted toward Rachel. As he spoke with her, Viola spotted Amy— Oliver's girlfriend—sneak into the room. Amy scanned the crowd until she saw Oliver filling champagne glasses at one of the tables. Amy sauntered to him and tapped him on the shoulder. Obviously happy to see her, he kissed her on the lips.

Oliver checked his watch. Viola knew Amy must have asked him how much longer he had to work. The reception had begun later than expected, but now that all the food had been served and the evening was almost over, Viola had no qualms about letting Oliver go early. He'd done so much for her and her mother. He deserved to be able to spend New Year's Eve with his girlfriend.

For some reason, Viola's eyes traveled over to Jonas at this thought. Jonas wasn't looking back at her. Instead, he was focused on Oliver and Amy. His brows pulled together.

In the next moment, Oliver made his way toward Viola.

"Viola, I was wondering—"

"You can go." Viola smiled at him. "You were great today. Thank you for all your assistance."

"Are you sure you don't need me anymore?"

"You've surpassed your obligations, so yes." Viola lowered her voice. "So, you're going to pop the question?"

Oliver's cheeks grew crimson. "If I can get the nerve up."

"That's so exciting. Good luck. And Happy New Year."

Oliver nodded, emitting a nervous laugh. "Happy New Year." He held up a finger to let Amy know he needed a minute and then disappeared into the kitchen to get his things.

Viola's attention went back to Jonas. This time, his green eyes were locked on her.

When he began walking in her direction, Viola panicked and slipped into the kitchen.

What is he doing? Hasn't he made me feel bad enough?

She pulled her ponytail tighter and scanned the kitchen, hoping to make it seem like she was too busy to be interrupted in case Jonas came into the kitchen to talk to her.

She grabbed a rag and wiped down the counter. Jonas entered the kitchen, and Viola felt a rock in the pit of her stomach. Christelle, who was at the sink, looked over at Jonas and then Viola.

Viola cleared her throat. "Yes, Mr. Brickman, can I help you?"

"Mr. Brickman, huh?" Jonas stuck his hands in his pockets. "I guess I deserved that."

"I don't know what you mean."

He rubbed at the space between his nose and mouth. "Did you hear about what happened out there? The wedding crasher?"

"Yeah." She still avoided looking at him, cleaning the counter even though it was spotless. "I heard you helped save the guy."

"No. I mean, I had some rope …" He trailed off.

Viola supposed her refusal to face him had irritated him so sufficiently that he decided not to continue his story. *Good. I hope he leaves.*

She swallowed hard, trying to convince herself that she wanted him to walk away, even though her heart wanted him to stay.

He took three steps closer. "I, uh, thought I should update you— I mean, in case you were wondering—on my plans. My business plans, I mean. And my personal plans, I guess."

The delivery of his words was dizzying. She narrowed her eyes and finally looked at him. "What are you saying? I can't follow."

He rubbed the back of his neck. "I thought maybe you'd like to know that I decided to remain in Silverwood after all."

"But you said you're moving to Billings. Selling the chateau."

He searched her face. "I changed my mind."

"And what brought about this change?"

He grimaced. "Let's say I didn't have all the necessary information to base my decision on."

"And now you do?"

"I think so."

Viola scoffed. "Jonas, you're confusing me. That doesn't sound like you: making important business decisions and then suddenly changing your mind. And why, exactly, are you telling me this anyway?"

"Because the information I was missing was the fact that you are single and not engaged to that waiter."

Viola blinked, shaking her head. She opened her mouth to speak, but her thoughts hadn't yet caught up with her vocal cords.

"S-Single?" she repeated. "What, uh …"

Christelle wiped her hands on a towel. "Why don't I give you two a minute?"

As soon as Christelle left the kitchen, Viola gaped at Jonas. He bit the inside of his cheek and stepped nearer to her.

Viola crossed her arms. "So, you thought that I was engaged to Oliver?"

"I walked into the dining hall before, and I saw him holding an open ring box to you, and then you hugged him, and then I couldn't breathe anymore."

A small grin tugged at her lips. "And that upset you so much that you decided to sell your business and move to Billings?"

He averted his gaze for a second. When he looked up at her again, his eyes were intense. "Yes."

"So you were jealous."

"I … was."

Her skin tingled, and she felt slightly lightheaded. "I see." She uncrossed her arms and closed the distance between them. "You're staying in Silverwood?"

"Turns out I have good reason to stay here. I mean, if I'm wanted."

Her smile grew. "Well, then, it's a good thing I'm not engaged to Oliver."

Jonas reached up and ran his thumb down the side of her face. "It's a very good thing."

Viola's heart drummed as Jonas leaned in. She tilted her head up, letting their lips drift together into a kiss as sweet as pie.

Chapter Twenty-Eight

Kim had been hugging Holly for what seemed like endless minutes, not showing any signs of letting go.

"You're going to miss your flight," Holly said over Kim's shoulder.

"I don't care," Kim whined. "I still have to meet my mountain man anyway."

Holly's laugh was crushed by Kim's embrace. "Well, then, you have a good reason to come back for a visit."

Kim finally released her. "I'll definitely be back."

She held her arms out to Nick, who had been waiting patiently nearby. Holly could almost see the fear in his eyes as Kim dragged him in for a hug.

Cupid paced around them, glancing up at Nick to check that he wasn't being attacked.

"Nicky, you're amazing. You and Holly are so perfect together." Kim stepped back and tilted her head. "Thank you for everything."

"Thank you for coming," Nick replied. "I know it wouldn't have been the same without you, and I'm pretty sure you've got an open invitation to come back."

"I'll give you a heads-up so you can maybe round up some of your best-looking single buds to, uh, keep me entertained."

Nick nodded. "You've got it."

Kim extended the handle of her rolling carry-on. "All right, you crazy kids, I'm off. Happy New Year. Love you."

Blowing kisses before she turned, Kim strutted off toward her gate.

"Well." Nick put his arm around Holly. "Silverwood's going to be much quieter now."

Holly playfully elbowed him, but she had to agree.

Holly's suitcase lay open on the bed. Packing shorts, tank tops, and bathing suits felt strange when it was snowing outside.

In the evening, she and Nick would be flying to Jamaica for their honeymoon, but first, they had to drop off her mom for her flight back to the Philippines. Holly felt like a regular at the airport, having just taken Kim a few days prior.

Holly went into the hall and peeked into her mom's room. She caught Vivian placing cash under a candlestick holder.

"Mom, what are you doing?"

Vivian jumped at the sound of Holly's voice. "You scared me."

"Sorry. But why are you putting money on the dresser? I can't decipher what kind of message you're trying to send."

Vivian laughed. "No. I can't use dollars. You keep them."

"You could hold on to them for your next visit."

"But I don't know when that will be."

"Don't say that." Holly frowned. "It'll make me sad. Just say you'll be back soon."

Vivian hugged her. "I'll be back soon."

The sound of the front door opening broke their embrace.

"Nick's home."

Holly and Vivian made their way to the living room. Cupid ran up to greet them, sniffing and panting, happily wagging his tail.

Vivian crouched to pet him. "Oh, I'm going to miss you, too, my friend. Thanks for keeping my feet warm every night. I'd invite you to come with me, but it would be way too hot for you."

As Vivian cuddled with Cupid, Holly made a beeline for Nick. "Hello, Husband."

Nick pulled Holly close and pecked her lips. "Hello, Wife."

"Did you and Cupid have a nice walk?" Holly asked.

"Yes, but someone missed you too much and had to come back."

"Aww, well, I missed Cupid too," Holly joked.

"Ha ha." Nick kissed her once more before releasing her. "Vivi, can I get your bags?"

"Thank you, Nick. They're in the bedroom. All ready to go."

"Yes, ma'am. My pleasure."

The ride to the airport went way too fast for Holly. Her mother had been in Silverwood for weeks, but Holly felt like she had been too busy to have fully enjoyed her visit. After parking and checking Vivian in, Holly wasn't quite ready to say goodbye.

"It's a shame we live so far away from each other." Holly embraced her mom. "Hasn't anyone invented a teleporter yet so we could just be transported to each other's places in the blink of an eye?"

"That would be a dream come true." Vivian laughed. "Then again, you know us older folks and technology. I'd probably complain about not knowing which button to push and end up in the wrong place."

Cupid sat watching them. He nuzzled Vivian's leg with his snout and then placed a paw on her to get her attention. In response, she bent over and scratched between his ears.

"I'm so glad you were able to come, Mom." She took her hand and squeezed it. "Please don't wait years before you visit again."

"You two could come visit me," Vivian suggested.

"We'd love that." Nick smiled at her. "I've always wanted to see Asia. We could make a tour of it."

"And you could join us," Holly added.

"Sounds lovely. Sign me up." Vivian let out a chuckle. "Well, I hate goodbyes, so I'm going to get to my gate before I start crying."

At the mere sound of the word, Holly's eyes welled up. "I love you, Mom. Have a safe flight."

Vivian hugged Nick. "Thank you for bringing love into my daughter's life. You make her very happy."

"I'm honored to do so. For the rest of our lives."

Vivian patted his shoulder. "Good to hear."

Cupid barked.

"Goodbye to you, too." Vivian rubbed his head, turned to Holly, and hugged her once more. "Bye, my darling. I love you."

Nick draped his arm around Holly as Vivian took a step back.

"I'll text you when I'm settled in back home," Vivian said. "In the meantime, you two could start on those grandchildren you promised me."

"Mom!" Holly blushed.

"Bye."

Vivian made her way to her gate, turning to wave occasionally. Holly waited until she was out of sight, with Nick at her side and Cupid at her feet. Though the moment felt sad, Holly knew she was blessed—blessed that she was able to have her mother there to experience her special day and blessed to have married the love of her life. And she knew that if she concentrated on counting her blessings, there would be no time to worry about anything else.

Acknowledgements

In the time that occurred between me writing this story and editing it, I suffered two devastating losses. My two Siberian huskies had been diagnosed with tumors. They were both getting older, and I knew that time would catch up with them, but I didn't know it would all happen so quickly. We lost them both within three months of each other, and after having them for over ten years, I found it extremely difficult to get used to live without them. They were always there when I woke up in the morning, when I came home from work, and when I'd sit down with my family in the living room, they would join us for a cuddle or to beg for us to play with them. But then suddenly, they were gone. They were basically around for my entire writing career so far, and I want to extend thanks to them, just for being there and filling my life with love and joy.

I also want to thank everyone who was involved in putting this story together and polishing it so it can shine. Of course, I couldn't do any of this without the support of my friends and family, and I want to thank my readers, old and new.

About the Author

Dorothy Dreyer is an award-winning, USA Today bestselling author. Born in Angeles City, Philippines to a Filipino mother and American Father, Dorothy grew up a military brat, living in Guam, Massachusetts, South Dakota, New Jersey, and New York. Dorothy is bilingual, speaking fluent English and German, and teaches English to children at a multilingual school in Frankfurt, Germany, where she resides with her family. She always has a story or two running through her brain, and she loves to share those stories with anyone willing to listen.

www.DorothyDreyer.com